T0144782

Miss Numè of Japan

Miss Numè of Japan

A Japanese-American Romance

Onoto Watanna

MINT EDITIONS

Miss Numè of Japan: A Japanese-American Romance was first published in 1899.

This edition published by Mint Editions 2021.

ISBN 9781513208718 | E-ISBN 9781513276540

Published by Mint Editions®

MINT
EDITIONS
minteditionbooks.com

Publishing Director: Jennifer Newens
Design & Production: Rachel Lopez Metzger
Project Manager: Micaela Clark
Typesetting: Westchester Publishing Services

Contents

I

Parental Ambitions

When Orito, son of Takashima Sachi, was but ten years of age, and Numè, daughter of Watanabe Omi, a tiny girl of three, their fathers talked quite seriously of betrothing them to each other, for they had been great friends for many years, and it was the dearest wish of their lives to see their children united in marriage. They were very wealthy men, and the father of Orito was ambitious that his son should have an unusually good education, so that when Orito was seventeen years of age, he had left the public school of Tokyo and was attending the Imperial University. About this time, and when Orito was at home on a vacation, there came to the little town where they lived, and which was only a very short distance from Tokyo, certain foreigners from the West, who rented land from Sachi and became neighbors to him and to Omi.

Sachi had always taken a great deal of interest in these foreigners, many of whom he had met quite often while on business in Tokyo, and he was very much pleased with his new tenants, who, in spite of their barbarous manners and dress, seemed good-natured and friendly. Often in the evening he and Omi would walk through the valley to their neighbors' house, and listen to them very attentively while they told them of their home in America, which they said was the greatest country in the world. After a time the strange men went away, though neither Sachi nor Omi forgot them, and very often they talked of them and of their foreign home. One day Sachi said very seriously to his friend:

"Omi, these strangers told us much of their strange land, and talked of the fine schools there, where all manner of learning is taught. What say you that I do send my unworthy son, Orito, to this America, so that he may see much of the world, and also become a great scholar, and later return to crave thy noble daughter in marriage?"

Omi was fairly delighted with this proposal, and the two friends talked and planned, and then sent for the lad.

Orito was a youth of extreme beauty. He was tall and slender; his face was pale and oval, with features as fine and delicate as a girl's.

His was not merely a beautiful face; there was something else in it, a certain impassive look that rendered it almost startling in its wonderful inscrutableness. It was not expressionless, but unreadable—the face of one with the noble blood of the Kazoku and Samourai—pale, refined, and emotionless.

He bowed low and courteously when he entered, and said a few words of gentle greeting to Omi, in a clear, mellow voice that was very pleasing. Sachi's eyes sparkled with pride as he looked on his son. Unlike Orito, he was a very impulsive man, and without preparing the boy, he hastened to tell him at once of their plans for his future. While his father was speaking Orito's face did not alter from its calm, grave attention, although he was unusually moved. He only said, "What of Numè, my father?"

Sachi and Omi beamed on him.

"When you return from this America I will give you Numè as a bride," said Omi.

"And when will that be?" asked Orito, in a low voice.

"In eight years, my son, and you shall have all manner of learning there, which cannot be acquired here in Tokyo or in Kyushu, and the manner of learning will be different from that taught anywhere in Japan. You will have a foreign education, as well as what you have learned here at home. It shall be thorough, and therefore it will take some years. You must prepare at once, my son; I desire it."

Orito bowed gracefully and thanked his father, declaring it was the chief desire of his life to obey the will of his parent in all things.

Now Numè was a very peculiar child. Unlike most Japanese maidens, she was impetuous and wayward. Her mother had died when she was born, and she had never had any one to guide or direct her, so that she had grown up in a careless, happy fashion, worshiped by her father's servants, but depending entirely upon Orito for all her small joys. Orito was her only companion and friend, and she believed blindly in him. She told him all her little troubles, and he in turn tried to teach her many things, for, although their fathers intended to betroth them to each other as soon as they were old enough, still Numè was only a little girl of ten, whilst Orito was a tall man-youth of nearly eighteen years. They loved each other very dearly; Orito loved Numè because she was one day to be his little wife, and because she was very bright and pretty; whilst Numè loved big Orito with a pride that was pathetic in its confidence.

That afternoon Numè waited long for Orito to come, but the boy had gone out across the valley, and was wandering aimlessly among the hills, trying to make up his mind to go to Numè and tell her that in less than a week he must leave her, and his beautiful home, for eight long years. The next day a great storm broke over the little town, and Numè was unable to go to the school, and because Orito had not come she became very restless and wandered fretfully about the house. So she complained bitterly to her father that Orito had not come. Then Omi, forgetting all else save the great future in store for his prospective son-in-law, told her of their plans. And Numè listened to him, not as Orito had done, with quiet, calm face, for hers was stormy and rebellious, and she sprang to her father's side and caught his hands sharply in her little ones, crying out passionately:

"No! no! my father, do not send Orito away."

Omi was shocked at this display of unmaidenly conduct, and arose in a dignified fashion, ordering his daughter to leave him, and Numè crept out, too stunned to say more. About an hour after that Orito came in, and discovered her rolled into a very forlorn little heap, with her head on a cushion, and weeping her eyes out.

"You should not weep, Numè," he said. "You should rather smile, for see, I will come back a great scholar, and will tell you of all I have seen—the people I have met—the strange men and women." But at that Numè pushed him from her, and declared she wanted not to hear of those barbarians, and flashed her eyes wrathfully at him, whereat Orito assured her that none of them would be half as beautiful or sweet as his little Numè—his plum blossom; for the word Numè means plum blossom in Japanese. Finally Numè promised to be very brave, and the day Orito left she only wept when no one could see her.

And so Orito sailed for America, and entered a great college called "Harvard." And little Numè remained in Japan, and because there was no Orito now to tell her thoughts to, she grew very subdued and quiet, so that few would have recognized in her the merry, wayward little girl who had followed Orito around like his very shadow. But Numè never forgot Orito for one little moment, and when every one else in the house was sound asleep, she would lie awake thinking of him.

II

CLEO

"N o use looking over there, my dear. Takie has no heart to break—never knew a Jap that had, for that matter—cold sort of creatures, most of them."

The speaker leaned nonchalantly against the guard rail, and looked half-amusedly at the girl beside him. She raised her head saucily as her companion addressed her, and the willful little toss to her chin was so pretty and wicked that the man laughed outright.

"No need for *you* to answer in words," he said. "That wicked, willful look of yours bodes ill for the Jap's—er—heart."

"I would like to know him," said the girl, slowly and quite soberly. "Really, he is very good-looking."

"Oh! yes—I suppose so—for a Japanese," her companion interrupted.

The girl looked at him in undisguised disgust for a moment.

"How ignorant you are, Tom!" she said, impatiently; "as if it makes the slightest difference *what* nationality he belongs to. Mighty lot *you* know about the Japanese."

Tom wilted before this assault, and the girl took advantage to say: "Now, Tom, I want to know Mr.—a—a—Takashima. *What* a name! Go, like the dear good boy you are, and bring him over here."

Tom straightened his shoulders.

"I utterly, completely, and altogether *refuse* to introduce you, young lady, to any other man on board this steamer. Why, at the rate you're going there won't be a heart-whole man on board by the time we reach Japan."

"But you said Mr. Ta—Takashima—or 'Takie,' as you call him, had no heart."

"True, but you might create one in him. I have a great deal of confidence in you, you know."

"Oh! Tom, *don't* be ridiculous now. Horrid thing! I believe you just want to be coaxed."

Tom's good-natured, fair face expanded in a broad smile for a moment. Then he tried to clear it.

"*Always* disliked to be coaxed," he choked.

"Hem!" The girl looked over into the waters a moment, thinking. Then she rose up and looked Tom in the face.

"Tom, if you don't I'll go over and speak to him without an introduction."

"Better try it," said Tom, aggravatingly. "Why, you'd shock him so much he wouldn't get over it for a year. You don't know these Japs as I do, my dear—dozens of them at our college—awfully strict on subject of etiquette, manners, and all that folderol."

"Yes, but I'd tell him it was an American custom."

"Can't fool Takashima, my dear. Been in America eight years now—knows a thing or two, I guess."

Takashima, the young Japanese, looked over at them, with the unreadable, quiet gaze peculiar to the better class Japanese. His eyes loitered on the girl's beautiful face, and he moved a step nearer to them, as a gentleman in passing stood in front, and for a moment hid them from him.

"He is looking at us now," said the girl, innocently.

Tom stared at her round-eyed for a moment.

"How on earth do you know that? Your head is turned right from him."

Again the saucy little toss of the chin was all the girl's answer.

"He's right near us now. Tom, please, please—now's your chance," she added, after a minute.

The Japanese had come quite close to them. He was still looking at the girl's face, as though thoroughly fascinated with its beauty. A sudden wind came up from the sea and caught the red cape she wore, blowing it wildly about her. It shook the rich gold of her hair in wondrous soft shiny waves about her face, as she tried vainly to hold the little cap on her head. It was a sudden wild wind, such as one often encounters at sea, lasting only for a moment, but in that moment almost lifting one from the deck. The girl, who had been clinging breathlessly to the railing, turned toward Takashima, her cheeks aflame with excitement, and as the violent gust subsided, they smiled in each other's faces.

Tom relented.

"Hallo! Takie—you there?" he said, cordially. "Thought you'd be laid up. You're a pretty good sailor, I see." Then he turned to the girl and said very solemnly and as if they had never even discussed the subject of an introduction, "Cleo, this is my old college friend, Mr. Takashima—Takie, my cousin, Miss Ballard."

"Will you tell me why," said the young Japanese, very seriously, "you did not want that I should know your cousin?"

"Don't mind Tom," the girl answered, with embarrassment, as that gentleman threw away his cigar deliberately; and she saw by his face that he intended saying something that would mislead Takashima, for he had often told her of the direct, serious and strange questions the Japanese would ask, and how he was in the habit of leading him off the track, just for the fun of the thing, and because Takashima took everything so seriously.

"Why—a—" said Tom, "the truth of the matter is—my cousin is a—a flirt!"

"Tom!" said the girl, with flaming cheeks.

"A flirt!" repeated the Japanese, half-musingly. "Ah! I do not like a flirt—that is not a nice word," he added, gently.

"Tom is just teasing me," she said; and added, "But how did you know Tom did not want you to know me?"

"I heard you tell him that you want to know me, and I puzzle much myself why he did not want."

"I was sorry for you in advance, Takie," said Tom, wickedly, and then seeing by the girl's face that she was getting seriously offended, he added: "Well, the truth is—er—Cleo—is—a so—young, don't you know. One can't introduce their female relatives to many of their male friends. You understand. That's how you put it to me once."

"Yes!" said Takashima, "I remember that I tell you of that. Then I am most flattered to know your relative."

As Tom moved off and left them together, feeling afraid to trust himself for fear he would make things worse, he heard the gentle voice of the Japanese saying very softly to the girl:

"I am most glad that you do not flirt. I do not like that word. Is it American?"

Tom chuckled to himself, and shook his fist, in mock threat, at Cleo.

III

Who Can Analyze a Coquette?

Cleo Ballard was a coquette; such an alluring, bright, sweet, dangerous coquette. She could not have counted her adorers, because they would have included every one who knew her. Such a gay, happy girl as she was; always looking about her for happiness, and finding it only in the admiration and adoration of her victims; for they *were* victims, after all, because, though they were generally willing to adore in the beginning, she nevertheless crushed their hopes in the end; for that is the nature of coquettes. Hers was a strange, paradoxical nature. She would put herself out, perhaps go miles out of her way, for the sake of a new adorer, one whose heart she knew she would storm, and then perhaps break. She would do this gayly, thoughtlessly, as unscrupulously and impetuously as she tore the little silk gloves from her hands because they came not off easily. And yet, in spite of this, it broke her heart (and, after all, she had a heart) to see the meanest, the most insignificant of creatures in pain or trouble. With a laugh she pulled the heart-strings till they ached with pain and pleasure commingled; but when the poor heart burst with the tension, then she would run shivering away, and hide herself, because so long as she did not see the pain she did not feel it. Who can analyze a coquette?

Then, too, she was very beautiful, as all coquettes are. She had sun-kissed, golden-brown hair,—dark brown at night and in the shadow, bright gold in the daytime and in the light. Her eyes were dark blue, sombre, gentle eyes at times, wicked, mischievous, mocking eyes at others. Of the rest of her face, you do not need to know, for when one is young and has wonderful eyes, shiny, wavy hair and even features, be sure that one is very beautiful.

Cleo Ballard *was* beautiful, with the charming, versatile, changeable, wholly fascinating beauty of an American girl—an American beauty.

And now she had a new admirer, perhaps a new—lover. He was so different from the rest. It had been an easy matter for her to play with and turn off her many American adorers, because most of them went into the game of hearts with their eyes open, and knew from the first that the girl was but playing with them. But how was she to treat one who believed every word she said, whether uttered gayly or otherwise, and who, in his gentle, undisguised way, did not attempt, even from the beginning, to hide from her the fact that he admired her so intensely?

Ever since the day Tom Ballard had introduced Takashima to her, he had been with her almost constantly. Among all the men, young and old, who paid her court on the steamer, she openly favored the Japanese. Most Japanese have their full share of conceit. Takashima was not lacking in this. It was pleasant for him to be singled out each day as the one the beautiful American girl preferred to have by her. It pleased him that she did not laugh or joke so much when with him, but often became even as serious as he, and he even enjoyed hearing her snub some of her admirers for his sake.

"Cleo," Tom Ballard said to her one day, as the Japanese left her side for a moment, "have mercy on Takashima; spare him, as thou wouldst be spared."

She flushed a trifle at the bantering words, and looked out across the sea.

"Why, Tom! he understands. Didn't you say he had lived eight years in America?"

Tom sighed. "Woman! woman! incorrigible, unanswerable creature!"

After a time Cleo said, almost pleadingly, as if she were trying to defend herself against some accusation:

"Really, Tom, he *is* so nice. I can't help myself. You haven't the slightest idea how it feels to have any one—any one like that—on the verge of being in love with you."

Takashima returned to them, and took his seat by the girl's side.

"To-night," he told her, "they are going to dance on deck. The band will play a concert for us."

Cleo smiled whimsically at his broken English, for, in spite of his long residence in America, he still tripped in his speech.

"Do you dance?" she asked, curiously.

"No! I like better to watch with you."

"But I dance," she put in, hastily.

Takashima's face fell. He looked at her so dejectedly that she laughed. "Life is so serious to you, is it not, Mr. Takashima? Every little thing is of moment."

He gravely agreed with her, looking almost surprised that she should consider this strange.

"We are always taught," he said, gently, "that it is the little things of life which produce the big; that without the little we may not have the big. So, therefore, we Japanese measure even the smallest of things just as we do the large things."

Cleo repeated this speech later to Tom, and an Englishman who had been paying her a good deal of attention. They both laughed, but she felt somewhat ashamed of herself for repeating it.

"I suppose, then, you will not dance," said the Englishman. Cleo did not specially like him. She intended fully to dance, that night, but a contrary spirit made her reply, "No; I guess I will not."

She glanced over to where the young Japanese sat, a little apart from the others. His cap was pulled over his eyes, but the girl felt he had been watching her. She recrossed the deck and sat down beside him.

"Will you be glad," she asked him, "when we reach Japan?"

A shadow flitted for a moment across his face before he replied.

"Yes, Miss Ballard, most glad. My country is very beautiful, and I wish very much to see my home and my relations again."

"You do not look like most Japanese I have met," she said, slowly, studying his face with interest. "Your eyes are larger and your features more regular."

"That is very polite that you say," he said.

The girl laughed. "No! I didn't say it for politeness," she protested, "but because it is true. You are really very fine looking, as Tom would say;" she halted shyly for a moment, and then added, "for—for a Japanese."

Takashima smiled. "Some of the Japanese do not have very small eyes. Very few of the Kazoku class have them. That it is more pretty to have them large we do not say in Japan."

"Then," said the girl, mischievously, "you are not handsome in Japan."

This time Takashima laughed outright.

"I will try and be modest," he said. "Therefore, I will let *you* be the judge when we arrive there. If you think I am, as you say, handsome, then shall I surely be."

IV

The Dance on Deck

That evening the decks presented a gala appearance. On every available place, swung clear across the deck, were Japanese and Chinese lanterns and flags of every nation. The band commenced playing even while they were yet at dinner, and the strains of music floated into the dining-room, acting as an appetizer to the passengers, and giving them anticipation of the pleasant evening in store. About seven o'clock the guests, dressed in evening costume, began to stroll on deck, and as the darkness slowly chased away the light, the pat of dainty feet mingled with the strains of music, the sough of the sea and the sigh of the wind. Lighted solely by the moon and the swinging lanterns, the scene on deck was as beautiful as a fairyland picture.

Cleo Ballard was not dancing. She was sitting back in a sheltered corner with Takashima. Her eyes often wandered to the gay dancers, and her little feet at times could scarcely keep still. Yet it was of her own free will that she was not dancing. When she had first come on deck she was soon surrounded with eager young men ready to be her partners in the dance. The girl had stood laughingly in their midst, answering this one with saucy wit and repartee, snubbing that one (when he deserved it), and looking nameless things at others. And as she stood there laughing and talking gayly, a girl had passed by her and made some light remark. She did not catch the words. A few moments after she saw the same girl sitting alone with Takashima, and there was a curiously stubborn look about Cleo's eyes when she turned them away.

"Don't bother me, boys," she said. "I don't believe I want to dance just yet. Perhaps later, when it gets dark. I believe I'll sit down for a while anyhow."

She found her way to where Takashima and Miss Morton were sitting. Miss Morton was talking very vivaciously, and the Japanese was answering absently. As Cleo came behind him and rested her hand for a moment on the back of his deck-chair, he started.

"Ah, is it you?" he said, softly. "Did you not say that you would dance?"

"It is a little early yet," the girl answered. "See, the sun has not gone down yet. Let us watch it."

They drew their deck-chairs quite close to the guard-rail, and watched the dying sunset.

"It is the most beautiful thing on earth," said Cleo Ballard, and she sighed vaguely.

The Japanese turned and looked at her in the semi-darkness.

"Nay! *you* are more beautiful," he said, and his face was eloquent in its earnestness. The girl turned her head away.

"Tell me about the women in Japan," she said, changing the subject. "Are not they very beautiful?"

Takashima's thoughtful face looked out across the ocean waste. "Yes," he said slowly; "I have always thought so. Still, none of them is as beautiful as you are—or—or—as kind," he added, hesitatingly.

The man's homage intoxicated Cleo. She knew all the men worth knowing on board—had known many of them in America. She had tired, bored herself, flirting with them. It was a refreshment to her now to wake the admiration—the sentiment—of this young Japanese, because they had told her he always concealed his emotions so skillfully. Not for a moment did she, even to herself, admit that it was more than a mere passing fancy she had for him. She could not help it that he admired her, she told herself, and admiration and homage were to her what the sun and rain is to the flowers. That Takashima could never really be anything to her she knew full well; and yet, with a woman's perversity, she was jealous even at the thought that any other woman should have the smallest thought from him. It is strange, but true, that a woman often demands the entire homage and love of a man she does not herself actually love, and only because of the fact that he does love her. She resents even the smallest wavering of his allegiance to her, even though she herself be impossible for him. It was because she fancied she saw a rival in Miss Morton that for a moment she became possessed of a wish to monopolize him entirely, so long as she would be with him.

When Miss Morton, who soon perceived that she was not wanted, made a slight apology for leaving them, Cleo turned and said, very sweetly: "Please don't mention it."

V

HER GENTLE ENEMY

Enemies are often easier made than friends. Fanny Morton was not an agreeable enemy to have. She was one of those women who were constantly on the look-out for objects of interest. She was interested in Takashima, as was nearly every one who met him. In the first place, Takashima was a desirable person to know; a graduate of Harvard University, of irreproachable manners, and high breeding, wealthy, cultured, and even good-looking. Moreover, the innate goodness and purity of the young man's character were reflected in his face. In fact, he was a most desirable person to know for those who were bound for the Land of Sunrise. That he could secure them the entrée to all desirable places in Japan, they knew. For this reason if for no other Takashima was popular, but it was more on account of the genuineness of the young man, and his gentle courtesy to every one, that the passengers sought him out and made much of him on the steamer. And it was partly because he was so popular that Cleo Ballard, with the usual vanity of woman, found him doubly interesting. In his gentle way he had retained all of them as his friends, in spite of the fact that he had attached himself almost entirely to Miss Ballard. On the other hand, the girl had suffered a good deal from the malicious jealousy of some of the women passengers, who made her a target for all their spite and spleen. But she enjoyed it rather than otherwise.

"Most people do not like me as well as you do, Mr. Takashima," she said once. He had looked puzzled a moment, and she had added, "That is because I don't like everybody. You ought to feel flattered that I like you."

Fanny Morton could not forgive Cleo the half-cut of the evening of the hop. A few days afterwards she said to a group of women as they lay back in their deck-chairs, languidly watching the restless waves, "I wonder what Cleo Ballard's little game is with young Takashima?"

She had told them of the conversation on deck, of the young Japanese's peculiar familiarity and homage in addressing her, and of the flowery, though earnest, compliments he had paid her.

"She must be in love with him," one of the party volunteered.

"No, she is not," contradicted an old acquaintance of Cleo's, "because Cleo could not be in love with any one. The girl never had any heart."

"I thought she was engaged to Arthur Sinclair, and was going out to join him in Tokyo," put in an anxious-looking little woman who had spent almost the entire voyage on her back, being troubled with a fresh convulsion of seasickness every time the sea got the least bit rough. It is wonderful what a lot of information is often to be got out of one of these invalids. During the greater part of the voyage they merely listen to all about them, and, as a rule, the rest are inclined to regard them as so many dummies. Then, toward the close of the voyage, they will surprise you with their knowledge on a question that has never been settled.

"That *is* news," said Cleo's old acquaintance, sitting up in her chair, and regarding the little woman with undisguised amazement. "Who told you, my dear?"

"I thought I heard her discussing it with her cousin the other day," the woman answered, with visible pleasure that she was now an object of interest.

"My dear," repeated the old acquaintance once more, settling her ample form in the canvas chair, "really, I must have been stupid not to have guessed this. Why, of course, I understand now. That was what all that finery meant in Washington, I suppose. That is why her mother has been so mysteriously uneasy about Cleo's—and I must say it now—outrageous flirtation with the Japanese. Every time she has been able to come on deck—and, poor thing, it has not been often through the voyage so far—she has called Cleo away from Mr. Takashima, and I've even heard her reprove her, and remonstrate with her. Well! well!"

Fanny Morton was smiling as she stole away from the party.

VI

A Veiled Hint

Always, after dinner, the young Japanese would come on deck, having generally finished his meal before most of the others, and rarely sitting through the eight or ten courses. Like the rest of his countrymen, he was a passionate lover of nature. Sunsets are more beautiful at sea, when they kiss and mirror their wonderful beauty in the ocean, than anywhere else, perhaps.

Fannie Morton found him in his favorite seat—back against a small alcove, his small, daintily manicured fingers resting on the back of a chair in front of him.

She pulled a chair along the deck, and sat down beside him.

"You are selfish, Mr. Takashima," she said, "to enjoy the sunset all alone."

"Will you not enjoy it also?" he asked, quite gravely. "I like much better, though," he continued, seeing that she had come up more to talk than to enjoy the sunset, "to look at the skies and the water rather than to talk. It is most strange, but one does not care to talk as much at sea as on land when the evenings advance."

"And yet," Miss Morton said, "I have often heard Miss Ballard's voice conversing with you in the evening."

The Japanese was silent a moment. Then he said, very simply and honestly, "Ah, yes, but I would rather hear her voice than all else on earth. She is different to me."

The girl reddened a trifle impatiently.

"Most men love flirts," she said, sharply.

The Japanese smiled quietly, confidently.

"Yes, perhaps," he said, vaguely, purposely misleading her.

Tom Ballard's hearty voice broke in on them.

"Well," he said, cheerfully, "thought I'd find Cleo with you, Takie," and then, smiling gallantly at Miss Morton, "but really, I see you've got 'metal more attractive.'" He winked, and continued, "Cousins are privileged beings. Can say lots of things no one else dare."

Fanny Morton's face brightened. She was a pretty girl, with pale brown hair, and a bright, sharp face.

"Oh, now, Mr. Ballard, you are flattering. What would Miss Cleo say?"

Tom scratched his head. "She would prove, I dare say, that I was—a—lying."

The play on words had been entirely lost on Takashima, who had become absorbed in his own reveries. Then Miss Morton's sharp words caught his ear, and he turned to hear what she was saying. She had mentioned the name of an old American friend of his, who had gone to Japan some years before.

"I suppose," Miss Morton had said, "she will be pretty glad when the voyage is over." She had paused here, and Tom had prompted her with a quick query, "Why?"

"Oh! for Arthur Sinclair's sake," she had retorted, and laughingly left them.

Casually, Tom turned to Takashima. "Remember Sinclair, Takie? Great big fellow at Harvard—in for all the races—rowing—everything going—in fact, all-round fine fellow?"

"Yes."

"Nice—fellow."

"Yes."

"Er—Cleo—that is, both Cleo and I, are old friends of his, you know."

Takashima's face was still enigmatical.

Cleo had had a headache that evening, and had returned to her stateroom after dinner. The water was rough, and few of the passengers remained on deck. Quite late in the evening, Tom went up. The sombre, silent figure of the Japanese was still there. He had not moved.

"Past eleven," Tom called out to him, and the gently modulated voice of the Japanese answered, "Yes; I will retire soon."

VII

JEALOUSY WITHOUT LOVE

T he next day Cleo rallied Takashima because he was unusually quiet, and asked him the cause. He turned and looked at her very directly.

"Will you tell me, Miss Ballard," he said, "why Mr. Sinclair will be so overjoyed that you come to Japan?"

The abrupt question startled the girl. She flushed a violent, almost angry red, and for a moment did not reply. Then she recovered herself and said: "He is a very dear friend of ours."

The Japanese looked thoughtfully at her. There was an embarrassed flush on her face. Again he questioned her very directly, still with his eyes on her face.

"Tell me, Miss Ballard, also, do you flirt only with me?"

Cleo's face was averted a moment. With an effort she turned toward him, a light answer on the tip of her tongue. Something in the earnest, questioning gaze of the young man held her a moment and changed her gay answer. Her voice was very low:

"No," she said. "Please don't believe that of me."

She understood that some one had been trying to poison him against her. Her eyes were dewy—with self-pity, perhaps, for at that moment the coquette in her was subdued, and the natural liking, almost sentiment, she had for Takashima was paramount. A silence fell between them. Takashima broke it after a while to say, very gently: "Will you forgive me, Miss Ballard?"

"There is nothing to forgive."

"Ah! yes," said Takashima, sadly, "because I have misjudged you so?" His voice was raised in a half-question. The girl's eyes were suffused.

"Let us not talk of it any more," he continued, noticing her distress and embarrassment. "I will draw your chair back here and we will talk. What will we talk of? Of America—of Japan? Of you—and of myself?"

"My life has been uninteresting," she said; "let us not talk of it to-night,—but tell me about yours instead. You must have some very pretty remembrances of Japan. Eight years is not such a long time, after all."

"No; that is true, and yet one may become almost a different being during that time." He paused thoughtfully. "Still, I have many beautiful remembrances of my home—all my memories, in fact, are sweet of it." Again he paused to think, and continued slowly: "I will also have beautiful memories of America."

"Yes, but they will be different," said the girl, "for, of course, America is not your home."

"One often, though, becomes homesick—let us call it—for a country which is not our own, but where we have sojourned for a time," he rejoined, quickly.

"Then, if Japan is as beautiful as they say it is, I will doubtless be longing for it when I return to America."

A flush stole to the young man's eager face.

"Ah! Miss Ballard, perhaps if you will say that when you have lived there a while, I might find courage to say that which I cannot say now. I would wish first of all to know how you like my home."

The girl put her hands at the back of her head, and leaned back in the deck-chair with a sudden nervous movement.

"Let us wait till then," she said, hastily. "Tell me now, instead, what is your most beautiful memory of Japan?"

"My pleasantest memory," he said, "is of a little girl named Numè. She was only ten years old when I left home, but she was bright and beautiful as the wild birds that fly across the valleys and make their home close by where we lived."

A flush had risen to the girl's face. She stirred nervously, and there was a slight faltering in her speech as she said: "Tom once told me of her—he said you had told him—that you had told him—you were betrothed to her."

She had expected him to look abashed for a moment, but his face was as calm as ever.

"I will not know that till I am home. My plans are unformed." He looked in her face. "They depend a great deal on *you*," he continued.

For a moment the girl's lips half-parted to tell him of her own betrothal, but she could not summon the courage to do so while he looked at her with such confidence and trust; besides, her woman's vanity was touched.

"Tell me about Numè," she said, and there was the least touch of pique in her voice.

"Her father and mine are neighbors, and very dear friends. I have known her all my life. When she was a little girl I used to carry her on my shoulders over brooks and through the woods and mountain passes, because she was so little, and I was always afraid she would fall and hurt herself."

Cleo was silent now. She scarcely stirred while the young man was speaking, but listened to him with strange interest. Takashima continued: "I used to tell her I would some day be her Otto (husband), and because she was so very fond of me that pleased her very much, and when I said so to our fathers, it pleased them also."

The girl was nervously twisting her little handkerchief into odd knots. She was not looking at Takashima.

"How queer," she said, "that our childhood memories are sometimes so clear to us! We so often look back on them and think how—how absurd we were then. Don't you think there is really more in the past to regret than anything else?"

Takashima looked at her in surprise.

"No," he said; almost shortly, "I have nothing to regret."

"And yet," she persisted, "neither of you was old enough to—to care for the other truly." Her words were irrelevant, and she knew it.

"We were inseparable always," the young man answered. "We were children, both of us, but in Japan very often we are always children—always young in heart."

Cleo could not have told why she felt the sudden overwhelming rebellion against his allegiance to Numè, even though she knew only too well that Takashima's heart was safe in her own keeping. With a woman's perversity and delight in being constantly assured of his love for her in various ways, in dwelling on it to feed her vanity, and yes, in wishing to hear the man who loved her disclaim—even ridicule—one whom in the past he might have cared for, she said:

"Do you *love* her?"

"Love?" the Japanese repeated, dwelling softly on the word. "That is not the word now, Miss Ballard. I have only known its meaning since I have met you," he added, gently.

The girl's heart beat with a pleasurable wildness. It was sweet to hear these words from the lips of one who hesitated always so deferentially from speaking his feelings; from one who a moment before had filled her with a fear that, after all, another might interest him just as she had done; for coquettes are essentially selfish.

"You will not marry her?" she questioned, in a low voice.

She could not restrain the almost pleading tone that crept into her voice; for though she kept telling herself that they could never be anything to each other, and that she already loved another, yet, after all, was she so sure of her heart? The Japanese was silent. "That will depend," he said, slowly. "It is the wish of our fathers. They have always looked forward to it." His voice was very sad as he added: "Perhaps I should grow to love her. Surely, I would try, at least, to do my duty to my parents."

With a sudden effort the girl rose to her feet.

"It would be a cruel thing to do," she said, "cruel for her and for you. It would be fair to no one. You do not love; therefore, you should not marry her." Her beautiful eyes challenged him. A wild hope crept into the Japanese's heart that the girl must surely return his feeling for her, or she would not speak so. He was Americanized, and man of the world enough, to understand somewhat of these things. He purposely misled her, taking pleasure in the girl's evident resentment at his marriage with Numè.

"I would never marry a man I did not love," she continued. "No! I would have to love him with my whole heart."

"It is different in Japan," he said, quietly. "There we do not always marry for love, but rather to please the parents. We try always to love after marriage—and often we succeed."

"Your customs are—are—barbarous, then," Cleo said, defiantly. "We in America could not understand them."

There was a vague reproach now in her voice. The Japanese had risen also. He was smiling, as he looked at the girl. Perhaps she felt unconsciously the tenderness of that look, for she turned her own head away persistently.

"Miss Ballard," he said, softly,—"Miss Cleo—I do not disagree with you, after all, as you think. It is true, as you say—there should be no marriage without love."

"And yet you are willing to follow the ancient customs of your country," she said, half-pettishly—almost scornfully.

"I did not say that," he said, smiling.

"Yes, but you make one believe it," she said.

"I did not mean to. I wanted only that you should believe that it might be so for my father's sake, if—if the one I did love was—impossible to me." There was a piercing passion in his voice that she had not thought him capable of.

One of those inexplicable, sudden waves of gentleness and tenderness that sometimes sweep over a woman, came over her. She turned and faced Takashima with a look on her face that would have made the coldest lover's heart throb with delight and hope.

"You must be always sure—always sure she is—she is impossible."

She was appalled at her own words as soon as they were uttered.

The Japanese had taken a step nearer to her. He half held his hands out.

"I am going below," she said, with sudden fright, "I—I—indeed, I don't know what I'm talking about."

VIII

The Man She Did Love

When she reached her stateroom, she threw herself on the couch, being overcome by a sudden weakness. She could not understand nor recognize herself. It was impossible that she was in love with Takashima, for she already loved another; and yet she could not understand why she should feel so keenly about Takashima, nor why it hurt her,—the idea of his caring for any one else. Was it merely the selfishness and vanity of a coquette? Cleo could scarcely remember a time, since she was old enough to understand that man was woman's natural plaything, that she had not thoughtlessly and gayly coquetted, flirted and led on all the men who had dared to fall in love with her. There was so seldom a real pang with her, because she had seldom permitted any affair to go beyond a certain length. That is, almost from the beginning she would let them know that her heart was not touched—that she was merely playing with them, because she could not help being a flirt. Then Arthur Sinclair had come into her life. As she thought of him a wonderful tenderness stole over her face, a tenderness that Takashima had never been able to call there.

It had been a case of love on her side almost from the first night they had met. But with the man it was different; and perhaps it was because of the fact that he at first had been almost indifferent to her, that the girl who had wearied of the over-attention of the other men, who had loved her unquestioningly, and whose love had been such an easy thing to win, specially picked him out as the one man to whom she could give her heart. How often it happens that she who has been loved and courted by every one, should actually love the only one who perhaps had been almost indifferent to her! True, Sinclair had paid her a good deal of attention from the beginning, but it was because he admired her solely on account of her beautiful face, and because she was popular everywhere with every one, and it touched his vanity that she should single him out.

Later, the girl's wonderful charm had grown on him; and one night when they stood on the conservatory balcony of her home, when the moon's kindly rays touched her head and lighted her face with an almost wild beauty, when the perfume of the roses in her breast and hair had stolen into his senses, and the great speaking eyes told the story of her heart, Sinclair had told her he loved her. He had told her so with a wild passion; had told her so at a time when, a moment before, he had not himself known it. That she was wonderfully beautiful he had always known, but he had thought himself proof against her. He was not. It came to him that night—the knowledge of an overmastering love for her that had suddenly possessed him—a love that was so unexpected and violent in its coming, that half of its passion was spent in that one glorious first night, when she had answered his passionate declaration solely by holding her hands out to him, and he had drawn her into his arms.

Sinclair had returned to his rooms that night almost dazed. Did he love her? he asked himself. A memory came back of the girl's wonderful beauty, of the love that had reflected itself in her eyes and had beautified them so. And yet he had seen her often so—she had always been beautiful, but before that he had been unable to call up anything more than strong admiration of her beauty. Was it not that he had drank too much wine that night? No! he seldom did that. It was the girl's beauty and the knowledge that she loved him that had turned his head; it was the wine too, perhaps, and the surroundings, the moonlight, the flowers, their fragrance—everything combined. And then, having thought confusedly over the whole thing, Arthur Sinclair had risen to his feet and walked restlessly up and down his room—because he was not sure of his own heart after all.

Cleo Ballard had known nothing of this struggle he had had with himself. After that night he had been an ideal lover,—always considerate, gentle, and tender. The girl's imperious nature had melted under the great love that had come into her life. She ceased for a time to be a coquette. Then she was only a loving, tender woman.

It was hardly a month after this that Sinclair was appointed American Vice-Consul at Kyoto, Japan. He had told Cleo very gently of the appointment, and they had discussed their future together. It meant separation for a time, for Sinclair did not urge an early marriage, and Cleo Ballard was perhaps too proud to want it.

"We will marry," Sinclair had said, "when I am thoroughly established, when I have something to offer you—when I can afford to keep my wife as I would like to keep you."

The girl had answered with half-quivering lip: "Neither of us is poor now, Arthur;" and Sinclair had answered, hastily, "Yes, but I had better make a place in the world for myself first—get established, you see, dear. We don't need to hurry. We have lots of time yet."

Cleo had remained silent.

"When I am settled I will send for you to join me, dear," Sinclair had added, "if you are willing to come."

"Willing!" she had answered, with indignant passion. "Oh, Arthur, I am willing to go anywhere where you are."

Her mother's illness, soon after this, absorbed Cleo for a time, so that when Sinclair left her, the date of their marriage still remained unsettled.

That was three years before. Since then the girl had kept up an almost constant correspondence with Sinclair. His letters were like him, tender and loving, almost boyish in their tone of joyousness, for Sinclair liked his new home and position so much that he wanted to remain there altogether. He wrote to Cleo, asking if she would not now come to Japan and judge for them, and if she liked the country they would live there altogether; if not—they would return to America.

The girl's pride had long been roused in her, and but for her love for Sinclair she might have given him up long before. But always the overmastering love she had for him kept her waiting, waiting on for him—waiting for him to send for her as he had promised he would. It is true, she had grown used to his absence, and often tried to console herself with the homage and love given by others, but it could not be—her heart turned always back to the man she had loved from the first, and even the little flirtations she indulged in were half-hearted. Sometimes Sinclair's letters showed a trace of haste and carelessness, often they were almost cold and perfunctory. At such times she would plunge into a round of reckless gayety, and try to forget for the time being her unsatisfied longing and love. And now she was on her way to join him. The voyage was long, and would have been tedious had it not been for Takashima. He gave her a new interest. Most of the other passengers she found uninteresting. Sinclair's last letters, although speaking of her trip, and seemingly urging her to come, appeared to her, sometimes, almost forced. The girl's proud, spoiled heart rebelled. It was with a feeling as much of hunger for sympathy and love, as of coquetry, that she had started her acquaintance with Takashima, and now as she lay in the narrow little couch in her room, she was asking her heart with a sudden fear whether her hunger for love had overpowered her. She was of a passionate, intense nature. It galled her always that she was separated from the man she loved,—that she could not at once have by her the love he had protested he felt for her. She buried her face in the pillows and sobbed bitterly. With a passionate nervousness, she thrust his picture away from her, and tried to think, instead, of Takashima, the gentle young Japanese who now loved her—not as Sinclair had done, with a passion of a moment that swept her from her feet, but with deference and respect, and yet with as strong a love as she could have desired.

IX

Merely a Woman

Even a woman in love can put behind her easily, for a time, the image of the one she at heart loves, when she replaces it with one for whom she cares (not, perhaps, in the same wild way as for the other, but with a sentiment that is tantamount to a flickering, wavering love—a love of a moment, a love awakened by gentle words—and perhaps put away from her after she has reasoned it out to herself); for it is true that the best cure for love is to try to love another.

Cleo Ballard was not heartless. She was merely a woman. That is why, half an hour after she had wept so passionately, she was smiling at her own beautiful face in the mirror, as she brushed her long wavy hair before it.

She was thinking of Takashima, and of his love for her, which he could not summon the courage to tell her of, and which she tried always to prevent his doing. There was a stubborn, half pettish look on her face when she thought of his possible love for "the Japanese girl."

"Even if I cannot be anything to him," she told herself, remorselessly, "still, if he does not love her, I'm doing both a kindness in preventing his marrying her."

She paused in her toilet, and sat down a moment to think.

"I can't analyze my own feelings," she said, half-fretfully. "I don't see why I should feel so—so bad at the idea of his—his caring for any one else. I am not in love with him. That is foolish. A woman cannot be in love with two men at once."

She smiled. "How strange! I believe it is true, though, and yet—and yet—if it is so—how differently I care for them!"

She rose again, and commenced twisting her hair up.

"Oh, how provoking it is! I don't believe there are many girls who would admit it—and yet it is true—that we can love one man and be 'in love' with another." She pushed the last pin into her hair impatiently. "I believe if it were not for the fact that he—that he—might really care for some one else—I'd give him up now, but somehow, as it is—Oh! how selfish—how mean I am!" She stopped talking to herself, and opening the door called out to her mother in the next room:

"Mother dear, are you dressing for dinner yet?"

The mother's weak voice answered: "No, dear; I shall not be at the table to-night."

"Oh, mother, I want you with me to-night," she said, regretfully, going into her mother's room.

"You want me *with* you?" said the mother, with mild astonishment. "Why, my dear, I thought—you usually like being alone—or—or with Mr.—er—with the Japanese."

"Not to-night, mother—not to-night," she said, and put her head down on her mother's neck with a half-caress, a habit she had had when a little girl, and which sometimes returned to her when in a loving mood.

"I don't understand myself to-night, mother," she whispered.

The peevish, nervous tones of the invalid mother repulsed her.

"My dear, *do* not ruffle my hair so—There! go on to the dining-room like a good girl. And *do*, dear, be careful. I am so afraid of your becoming too fond of this—this Japanese. You are always talking about him now, and Tom says you are inseparable on deck."

The girl raised her head, and rose from her kneeling posture beside her mother. There was a cold glint in her eyes.

"Really, mother, you need not fear for me," she said, coldly. "Tom only says things for the sake of hearing himself talk—you ought to know better than to mind him."

"We are so near Japan now," the mother said, peevishly, "and we have waited three years. I am not strong enough to stand anything like—like the breaking of your engagement now. My heart is quite set on Sinclair, dear—you must not disappoint me."

"Mother—I—," the girl commenced, in a pained voice, but the mother interrupted her to add, as she settled back in her pillows, "There, there, my dear, don't fly out at me—I understand—I really can trust you." There was a touch of tenderness mingled with the pride in the last hard words: "You always knew how to carry your heart, my dear."

The girl remained silent for a moment, looking bitterly at her mother; after awhile her face softened a trifle. She leaned over her once more and kissed the faded face. "Mother, mother—you really are fond of me, are you not?—let us be kinder to each other."

X

"Watching the Night"

It was quite a wistful, sad-faced girl who took her seat at the table, and answered, half absently, the light jests of some of the passengers.

Tom's sharp ears missed her usual merry tone. He glanced keenly at her, as she sat beside him, eating her dinner in almost absolute silence.

"What's up, Cleo?"

"Nothing, Tom."

"Don't fib, now. You are not in the habit of wearing such a countenance for nothing."

"I can't help my countenance, Tom," she rejoined, with just a suggestion of a break in her voice.

Tom looked at her a moment in silence, and then delicately turned his head away. After dinner he took her arm very affectionately, and they strolled out on deck together.

Takashima was sitting alone, as they came out. He was waiting for Cleo, as usual, and had been watching the door of the dining-room expectantly. Tom drew her off in a different direction from where the Japanese was sitting. For a short time they walked up and down the deck, neither of them speaking a word. Then Tom broke the silence, saying carelessly, as he lit a cigar:

"Mind my smoking, sis?"

"No, Tom," the girl answered, looking at him gratefully. Instinctively she felt the ready sympathy he always extended to her, often without even knowing her trouble, and seldom asking for her confidence. When she was worried or distressed about anything, Tom would take her very firmly away from every one, and if she had anything to tell she usually told it to him; for since they had been little girl and boy together Tom had been the recipient of all her woes. When he was a little boy of twelve, his father and mother both having died, Cleo's father, his uncle, had taken him into his family, and the two children had been brought up together. After the death of his uncle he had stood to the mother and Cleo as father, brother, and son in one, and they both became very dependent on him. Once in a while when he was feeling exceptionally loving to Cleo he would call her "little sis." That night he did so very lovingly.

"Feeling blue, little sis?" he asked.

"Yes, Tom."

Tom cleared his throat. "Er—er—Takashima?"

"No, Tom—it is not he. It is mother."

Tom stopped in his walk, and made a half-impatient exclamation.

"Oh, Tom, I do want to love her so much—but—but she won't let me. I mean—she is fond of me, and—and—proud, I suppose, but whenever I try to get close to her she repulses me in some way. We ought to be a comfort to each other, but—but there is scarcely any feeling between us." She caught her breath. "Tom, I don't know what's the matter with me to-night. I—I—Oh, Tom, I do want a little sympathy so much."

The young man threw his lighted cigar away. He did not answer Cleo, but he drew her little hand closer through his arm. After a time the girl quieted down, and her voice had lost its restlessness when she said: "Dear Tom—you are so good."

They strolled slowly back in the moonlight to where Takashima was sitting. He was leaning over the railing, watching the dark waves beneath in their silvery, shimmering splendor, touched by the moon's rays. He turned as Tom called out to him:

"See a—a whale, Takie?"

"No; I was merely watching the—the night."

Cleo raised her head and smiled at Tom, both of them enjoying the Japanese's naive way of answering.

"I was watching the night," he repeated, "and thinking of Miss Cleo. We generally enjoy such sights together."

"Well, to-night I thought I had a lien on her for a change," Tom said. "Cleo is too popular to be monopolized by one person, you know."

The Japanese smiled—a happy, confident smile. It touched the girl, and she said, impetuously: "Tom, it always depends on who has the monopoly."

Tom answered with mock sternness: "Very well, madam; I leave you and Takie to the tender mercies of each other."

"Your cousin likes you very much, does he not?" the Japanese asked her, as Tom moved away.

"Yes; Tom is the best boy in the world. I don't know what I'd do without him." She leaned her head against the railing. His next quiet, meaning words startled her: "Would you wish to marry with him?" She laughed outright; for she perceived the first touch of jealousy he had shown in these words.

She lifted her little chin in its old saucy fashion.

"No—not if Tom was the only man in the world. It would be too much like marrying one's brother."

She smiled at the anxious face of the Japanese. He bent over her chair a moment, then he drew back and stood against the rail, in a still indecisive posture. The girl knew instinctively what he wanted to say. Perhaps it was because she was tired, and her heart was hungry for a little love, that she did not try to prevent him from speaking.

"This afternoon, Miss Ballard, your words gave me courage. Will you marry with *me?*" he asked.

The question was so direct she could not evade it. She must face it out now. Yet she could find no words to answer at first. The effort it had cost the Japanese to say this had made him constrained, for he had all the pride of a Japanese gentleman; and after all he was not so sure that the girl would accept him. He had been told it was customary in America to speak to the girl herself before speaking to the parents, and it was in a stiff, ceremonious way that he did so. He waited silently for her answer.

"Don't let us talk about—about such things," she said; and again there was that little break in her voice that had been there when Tom had walked with her. "Our—our friendship has been so delightful," she added; "don't let us break it just now."

For the first time since she had known him there was a note of sternness in Takashima's voice.

"Love should not break friendship," he said. "It should rather cement it."

The wind blew her hair wildly about her face, and in her restlessness it irritated her. She put her hands up and held back the light, soft curls that had escaped.

"Shall I speak to your mother?" he asked her.

"No!—No!" she said, quickly; "mother has—has nothing to do with it."

"Will you not tell me what to expect, then?" The sadness of his voice touched the girl's heart, bringing the tears to her eyes.

"I cannot answer yet. Wait till we get to Japan. Please wait till then."

"I tried to plan ahead," he said, "but you are right, Miss Ballard. You will want some time to think this over. It will be but five days now before we reach Japan. If that you are very kind to me in those five days my heart shall take great hope of what your answer will be."

XI

AT THE JOURNEY'S END

Cleo Ballard could not have told what it was that made her so restless, almost feverish, during those remaining five days. She knew Takashima had meant to ask her to show in some way, during that time, just what he might expect. It was almost a prayer to her to spare him, if she knew it was in vain. But the girl was possessed, during those days, with an almost feverish longing for his companionship and sympathy. She showed it constantly when with him; she would look unspeakable longings into his eyes, longings she could not understand or analyze herself; she led him on to talk of his plans, and he even told her of some wherein he had counted on her companionship—how he would have a Japanese-American house—a home wherein both the beauty of Japan and the comfort of America would be combined; and of the trips they would take to Europe, and the friends they would make. He used the word "we" always, in speaking, and she never once questioned his right to do so. Often she herself grew so interested in his plans for the future that she made suggestions, and they laughed with light-hearted joyousness at the prospect. At the end of the five days Takashima had not even a lingering doubt left.

As the shores of his home came into view, and the passengers were all clustered on deck watching the speck of land in the offing grow larger and larger as they approached it, the young Japanese placed his hand firmly on Cleo's—so soft and slender—and said: "Soon we will reach home now—your home and mine."

A sudden vague fear crept into the girl's heart. She shivered as his hand touched hers, and there was a frightened, almost hunted, look in her eyes.

"Shall I have my answer now?" he continued.

Again she shivered. "Wait till we are on shore," she pleaded, "till we have rested; wait five more days—I must think—I—I—"

"Ah, Miss Cleo, yes, I will wait," he said, gently. "Surely, I can afford to do so. It is after all merely the formal answer I will ask for. These last days you have already answered me—with your beautiful eyes."

"Tom," the girl said, desperately, as the passengers were passing from the boat on to the dock below, and her cousin was tying the heavy straps around their loose baggage, "Oh, Tom—I am afraid now—I am afraid of—of Takashima."

Tom's usually sympathetic face was almost stern. He rose stiffly and looked at the girl remorselessly.

"I warned you, Cleo," he said; "I told you to be careful. You ought to have answered him directly five days ago, when he spoke to you. You are the greatest moral coward I know. I believe you could not summon pluck enough to refuse anybody. Don't know how you ever did. It is a wonder you are not engaged to a dozen at once."

XII

THOSE QUEER JAPANESE!

K yoto is by far the most picturesque city in Japan. It is situated between two mountains, with a beautiful river flowing through it. It is connected with Tokyo by rail, but the traveling accommodations are far from being as comfortable or commodious as in America; in fact, there are no sleeping-cars whatever, so that it is often matter of complaint among visitors that they are not as comfortable traveling by rail as they might be. It was in Kyoto that Sinclair and most of the Americans who visited Japan lived. Sinclair kept one office in Kyoto and another in Tokyo, and being inclined to shove most of his light duties on to his secretary, went back and forth between the two cities; in fact, he had a house in both places. Tokyo, with its immense population and its air of business and activity, is yet not so favored by foreigners, nor by the better class Japanese, as a place of residence as is Kyoto. Indeed, a great many of them carry on a business in Tokyo and also keep a house in Kyoto. Most of the merchants of Tokyo, however, prefer to live in one of the charming little villages a few hours' ride by train from Tokyo, on the shores of the Hayama, where there is a good view of Fuji-Yama, the peerless mountain. And it was almost under the shadow of this mountain that Takashima Orito and Numè had played together as children.

The Ballards took up their residence for the time being in the city of Tokyo, at an American hotel, where most of the other passengers who had arrived with them were staying. Arthur Sinclair had failed to meet them at the boat, though he sent in his place his Japanese secretary, who looked after their luggage for them, hailed jinrikishas, and saw them comfortably settled at the hotel, apologizing profusely for the non-appearance of Sinclair, and explaining that he had gone up to Kyoto the previous day, and had been delayed on important business.

When they were alone in their rooms the mother sank in a chair, complaining bitterly that Sinclair had failed to meet them.

"I will never get used to this—this strange place," she said, with her chronic dissatisfaction. "I won't be able to stay a week here. How could

Arthur Sinclair have acted so outrageously? I shall tell him just how I feel about it."

"Mother," Cleo turned on her almost fiercely, "you will say nothing to him. If he had something more important to attend to—if he did not want to come—we do not want him to put himself out for us—we do not care if he does not." Her voice reflected her mother's bitterness, however, and belied her words.

"He was always thoughtful," said Tom, laying his hand consolingly on his aunt's shoulder. "Come now, Aunt Beth, everything looks comfortable here—and I'm sure after we once get over the oddity of our surroundings we will find it quite interesting."

"It *is* interesting, Tom," said Cleo, from a window, "the streets are so funny outside. They are narrow as anything, and there are signboards everywhere."

Mrs. Ballard looked helplessly about the room.

"Tom, *what* do you suppose they will give us to eat? I have heard such funny tales about their queer cooking—chicken cooked in molasses, and—and raw fish—and—"

"Mother," put in the girl, impatiently, "this hotel is on the American plan. The little bell-boys and servants, of course, are Japanese—but everything will be as much like what we have at home as they can make it."

Both the mother and daughter were out of patience with everything and were tired, the mother being almost hysterical. Tom went over to her and tried to calm her down, talking in his easy, consoling way on every subject that would take her mind off Sinclair. After a time Mrs. Ballard's nervousness had quieted down, and she rested, her maid sitting beside her fanning her gently, while Tom and Cleo unpacked what luggage they had had in their staterooms with them, their other trunks not having arrived. The girl was feeling more cheerful.

"When I go back to America," she said, "I believe I'll take a little Japanese maid with me. They are so neat and amusing."

Tom looked at her gravely. "I thought you contemplated making your home here?" he quizzed.

"Perhaps I will," the girl said, saucily, "perhaps I won't. It depends on whether my mind changes itself."

"Hum!"

"Remember Jenny Davis, Tom?"

"Well, I guess so;—never saw you alone when she was in Washington."

"Well, she brought home with her the sweetest little Japanese maid you ever saw. She used to be—a—a geesa girl in Tokyo, and the people she worked for were horrid to her. So Jenny paid them some money and they let her bring—a—Fuka with her to America. Well, I wish you could have seen her. She wasn't bigger than that, Tom," measuring with her hand, "and she was just as cute as anything,—walks on her heels, and smiles at you even when you are offended with her, Jenny says."

"Where is Mrs. Davis now?" Tom asked. "Thought I heard some one say she had come back here."

"So she did. She is somewhere in Japan now. Last time I heard from her she was in Kyoto. I wrote her, care of Arthur though, because she moves around so much, and I told her we were coming. I half expected she would meet us." After thinking a moment she added, "Tom, do you know, there was not a single American to meet us? I think mamma is right (though I won't tell her so), and that Arthur acted abominably in not meeting us. It doesn't matter *what* business he had—he should have left it. He might at least have sent—a—a friend to meet us, instead of that smooth Japanese. Mrs. Davis says there is a perfect American colony here, and in Yokohama and Kyoto—they are scattered everywhere, and Arthur knows them all, and most of them know we are to be married."

"Sinclair's hands, I guess, are pretty full most of the time. Every American nearly that comes here pounces onto him. He wrote me once that he had a different party to dinner nearly every day at the Consulate—when he is in Kyoto, and I guess that is why the poor chap likes to run down here where every tourist does not throw himself at him. Sinclair never was a good—a—business man. Don't believe he has any idea of the responsibility of his work. Believe he'd just as lief throw it up, anyhow."

But, though Tom stood up for his friend, even he could not help feeling in himself that the girl was justly indignant.

XIII

Takashima's Home-Coming

Takashima had left the Americans at the dock. He had offered the Ballards every courtesy, even inviting them to go with him to his home. This, however, they refused, and as it had been so long since he had been in Japan he was almost as much a stranger to his surroundings as they were; so he left them to the care of Sinclair's secretary, feeling confident that he would show them every attention,—telling them that he would call on them the next day. He realized that they felt a trifle strange, and wanted, in his generous, gentle way, to make them feel at home in Japan. Two old Japanese gentlemen who stood on the dock, peering eagerly among the passengers as they passed down the gangway, now paused before him. Both were visibly affected, and the one who called his name so gently and proudly trembled while he did so.

"Orito, my son."

"My father," the young man answered, speaking, impulsively, in pure Japanese. With one old man holding each of his arms he moved away. Cleo looked after them, her beautiful eyes full of tears.

"It is his father," she had said. "They have not seen each other for eight years." Her voice faltered a trifle. "The other one must be *her* father."

XIV

AFTER EIGHT YEARS

It was with mingled feelings of pleasure and, perhaps, pain that Takashima Orito saw his home once more. The place had scarcely changed since he had left it eight years before. It seemed to him but a day since he and Numè had played on the shores of the Hayama, and had gathered the pebbles and shells on the beach. He remembered how Numè would follow him round wherever he went, how implicitly she believed in him. Surely, if he lived to be a hundred years old never would such confidence be placed in him again—the sweet, unquestioning confidence of a little child. After dinner Orito left his father and Omi to go outside the house and once more take a look at the old familiar scenes of his boyhood; once more to see Fuji-Yama, the wonderful mountain that he had known from his boyhood, and of which he had never tired. There it stood in its matchless lonely peace and splendor, its lofty peaks meeting the rosy beams of the vivid sky, snow-clad and majestic. Ah! the same weird influence, the same inexplicable feeling it had always produced in him had come back now, and filled his soul with an ardent, yearning adoration. Every nerve in the young man bespoke a passionate artistic temperament. Many a time when in America, wearied with studying a strange people, strange customs, and a strange God, his mind had reverted to Fuji-Yama—Fuji-Yama, the mount of peace, and in his heart would rise an uncontrollable longing to see it once more, for it is said that no one who is born within sight of Fuji-Yama ever forgets it. Though he might roam all the world over, his footsteps inevitably turn back to this spot. Standing majestically in the central part of the main island, snow-clad and solitary, surrounded by five lakes, it rises to the sublime altitude of 12,490 feet. It is said that its influence is almost weird—that those who gaze on it once must always remember it. They are struck not so much by its grandeur as by its wonderful simplicity and symmetry. It is suggestive of all the gentler qualities; it is symbolic of love, peace, and restfulness.

Orito remained outside the house for some time, his face turned in mute adoration to the peerless mountain, no sound escaping his lips.

When his father joined him he said, with a sigh: "Father, how came I ever to leave my home?"

The old man beamed on him, and leaned against his shoulder.

"Ah, my son, it pleases me much that you have found no spot more beautiful than your home. Most long have the days been without you. Tell me somewhat of your life in America."

"My father," the young man answered, "the world outside my home is turbulent and full of a restlessness that consumes the vitality of man and robs him of all peace." He pointed towards the mountain: "Here is rest, peace—Nirvana, rest from the pulse of the wild world."

The old man looked uneasy. "But, my son, surely you do not regret your travel?"

"No, father," said Orito. "Life is too short for regrets. It is folly to regret anything. Here in this land, where all is so beautiful, we sleep— perhaps a delicious, desirable sleep; but though there be beauty all about us, all that the heart could desire, the foolish heart of man still is not content. We cannot understand this restlessness that makes us want to leave the better things of life and go out into the world of sorrow, to leave beauty and rest behind us, and exchange it for a life of excitement, of shams and unrealities."

Old Sachi looked frightened at his son's words. He did not quite comprehend them, however. The son seemed to perceive this, and changed the subject quickly.

"Where is Numè, my father? I have not yet seen her. She must surely be a young lady now."

Once more the old man's face lighted up with pride and interest.

"I thought you would be tired after your long voyage, and would not care so much to see any one but your father. Therefore, when she desired to visit her American friends her father permitted her to do so." He smiled at his son. "You will see her to-morrow. She is now a young maiden, and you will not know her at first."

"No—perhaps not," the young man said, sadly. "I can think of her only as the little wild plum blossom of ten years. I shall not care for her as well now that she is a—perhaps—polite maiden of eighteen."

"You should rather like her better, now that she is a beautiful maiden instead of a mere baby, for it is the nature of man to prefer the woman to the child."

"Yes, I understand, father, but it is so many years since I have seen a Japanese girl, and I have grown more used to the American woman."

A shrewd look crept into the old man's face.

"Omi and I thought of that long ago, and for that reason we encouraged her to be with the Americans greatly, so that she has learned to speak their tongue, and often becomes almost as one of them."

"But, father, I would not wish her to be an American lady. She could not be—you cannot make a Japanese girl into an American girl. She would be more charming solely as a Japanese maid."

XV

Numè

The American lady with whom Numè was staying was the Mrs. Davis of whom Cleo Ballard had spoken. She had rented one of the houses that eight years before the foreigners had lived in. They had at that time filled the house with American furniture, so that when Mrs. Davis came to look at it, it had presented so familiar and homelike an appearance that she had rented it at once. She had lived there for some months now. In fact, as she was popular and always the centre of gay parties of foreigners, quite a small colony of Americans and English people had settled in that vicinity, which was within easy reach of Tokyo, and, indeed, only a day's journey from Kyoto. They had rented houses and land from Omi and Sachi, who cultivated them constantly because of their son. Mrs. Davis' husband was a large silk merchant in Tokyo, and they had practically made their home in Japan, though they often took trips to America and Europe.

Ever since Orito had left Japan Numè had lived a retired, reserved life. Although but a child at the time, she was of a peculiarly staunch and intense nature, and for many years after Orito had been gone, she clung to the memory of the happy days she had spent with him, and looked forward constantly to his return. With the usual unquestioning content of a Japanese girl, she was ready to marry whoever her father chose for her, so long as he was not repugnant to her; and as they had already decided on Orito, the girl took it as a matter of course that she would some day be his wife. As she had only pleasant memories of him, her marriage was looked forward to almost with delight, and until the day before Orito's return there had not been a pang of fear or regret. She had not been thrown into the society of young men, and knew very little of them. Orito's letters to her, although formal in tone, always were tender and kind, and spoke of the happy days they had spent together, and which he said would be renewed when he was once more in Japan.

When the Americans had settled so near her home, the girl had gone out curiously among them, studying their strange manners and customs, learning to speak their language, and often even dressing in their costume, to the amusement of her father, Sachi, and the Americans. They had sought her out in the beginning because of her extraordinary beauty; for, living on her father's land, they naturally often came across her either with her father or roaming alone with her maid in the fields. At first the child was inclined to resent any overtures on their part, because of an unaccountable jealousy she cherished toward them ever since Orito had gone to America. But after a time her better sense had triumphed, and soon she became a familiar figure in their midst.

It is true that most of these foreigners stayed only a short time there, and moved around constantly, but as fast as they went others came, and the girl soon got used to them. Although she had received the best education possible for a girl in Japan, yet she had traveled very little, her father taking her once in a while on a flying trip to Kyoto and Tokyo. But her knowledge of the outside world was gained entirely through her acquaintance with the Americans, and often she sighed for a larger life than the one she had known. She would ask her father constantly to permit her to go away on trips with the Americans, but though he encouraged her always to cultivate them, yet he never would permit her to go away with them, even on a short trip to Yokohama.

Omi was perhaps a trifle more limited and narrow than Sachi, and more regarded the etiquette of his class. Sachi had always been inclined to take the lead in most things, and Omi was always willing to be guided by him. Thus it happened that Omi had perhaps as much love for Orito as his father had, and even thought more of him than he did of Numè, who was only a girl.

Orito and Numè were the only children either of the old men had had, and, moreover, both of their mothers had died many years ago.

When Mrs. Davis had settled there about six months before, she had brought letters with her from Takashima Orito, whom she had met in America, commending her to the hospitality of his father and Omi. With her quick, gay manners, her beautiful and odd dresses, her frank good-nature, she dazzled and was a puzzle always to the old men and to Numè. Moreover, she was a wealthy woman, and had rented the most exquisite of all the houses owned by Sachi. She took a great liking to Numè almost at once, and the girl returned it. She would walk into Omi's house in the most insinuating manner in the world, captivate the old man with her wit and grace, and carry off Numè right under his nose, even though he had told her of his resolve to keep his daughter in seclusion until her marriage. She would say to him "Well, now, you know, Mr. Watanabe, I am different. I knew dear Mr. Takashima so well in America, and I am sure he would like Numè and me to be good friends, eh, Numè?" And when she was alone with the girl and out of sight of the old man, she would say, with a confident shake of her head: "Just wait, my dear; soon I'll have things so that you can come and go as you like."

She did not speak vainly. Soon she had taken the two old men by storm, so that she could have twisted them round her own shrewd little finger.

XVI

AN AMERICAN CLASSIC

The day before Orito was to arrive home Numè had crossed the rice fields and gone to the American lady's house.

"I have felt so nerviss," she said, with her pretty broken English, "that I come stay with you, Mrs. Davees."

"What are you nervous about, dear?" Mrs. Davis asked, kissing the girl's pretty, troubled face.

Numè slipped down from the chair Mrs. Davis had placed for her, and sat on the floor instead, resting her head against the older woman's knee.

"Orito will return to-morrow," she said, simply. "I am so joyed I am nerviss."

The American lady's sweet blue eyes were moist.

"Do you love him, sweetheart?"

The girl raised wondering eyes to her.

"Luf? Thad is so funny word—Ess—I luf," she said.

"And you have not seen him for eight years? And you were only ten years old when you last saw him? My dear, I don't understand—I can't believe it."

The girl raised a wistful face to her.

"Numè nod unerstan', too," she said.

"Of course you don't, dear. Numè, I wish your father would let me take you away for a time. It is a shame to tie you down already, before you have had a chance to see anything or any one, hardly. You aren't a bit like most Japanese girls. I don't believe you realize how pretty—how very, very lovely and dainty and sweet you are. Sometimes when I look at your face I can't realize you are a Japanese girl. You are so pretty."

"Bud the Japanese girl be pretty," Numè said, with dignity; "pretty more than Americazan girl," she added, defiantly.

Mrs. Davis laughed. "Yes, they are—I suppose, some of them, but then an American can't always understand their *style* of beauty, dear. You are different. Your face is lovely—it is a flower—a bright tropical flower. No! It is too delicate for a tropical flower—it is like your name— you *are* a wild plum blossom. Sometimes I am puzzled to know *when* you look best—in the sweet, soft kimona or—or in a regular stylish American gown; then I couldn't tell you were anything but an American girl;—no, not an American girl—you are too pretty even for that—you are individual—just yourself, Numè."

"The Americazan lady always flatter," the girl said, rising to her feet, her face flushed and troubled. "Japanese girl flatter too; Japanese girl tell you she thing' you vaery pritty—but she nod mean. Tha's only for polite. Thad you thing me pretty—tha's polite."

This speech provoked a hearty laugh from a gentleman reading a batch of letters at a small table.

"There's a lesson for you, Jenny. She can't jolly you, eh, Numè?"

"Numè nod unerstan' to jolly," the girl answered.

"Come here, Numè, and I'll tell you," he called across to her. She went over to his side, her little serious face watching him questioningly.

"A jollier is an American classical word, Numè—a jollier is one who jollies you."

"Numè *nod* unerstan', still."

Mrs. Davis drew Numè away from him.

"Leave her alone, Walter," she said, reprovingly; and then to the girl: "Numè, you must not believe a thing he tells you."

Walter Davis laid his paper-cutter down.

"Madam, are you teaching that young girl to lose faith in mankind already?"

Mrs. Davis answered by placing her little hand over his mouth and looking at him with her pretty blue eyes so full of reproach that he pulled her down beside him. They had been married only a little over eighteen months.

"Here is the literal translation of the word 'jolly,'" he said to Numè. "Now, I want Mrs. Davis to be in a good humor, so I squeeze her up and tell her she is the darlingest little woman in the world."

Still the girl's face was troubled. She looked at the husband and wife a moment; then she said, very shyly: "Numè lig' to jolly, too."

Mrs. Davis pushed her husband's arm away.

"Don't use that word—it is ugly. Walter is full of slang."

"Ess, bud," she persisted, "*if* thad the 'jolly' means to be *luf*, then I lig' thad liddle word."

"But you must not use the word, dear."

When Numè had gone to bed for the night, and husband and wife were alone together, Mrs. Davis reproached her husband.

"Really, Walter, I wish you would not teach that poor little thing such—a—a—wicked things—or—or that awful slang. First thing we know she will be using it seriously. You have no idea how quickly she catches on to the smallest new word, and she will ask more questions about it, if it catches her fancy, than a child of three."

"That's her charm, my dear," the man answered. "Ought to encourage it, Jen."

"She does not need *that* kind of a charm. She is a charm all by herself. Every movement she makes is charming, every halting word,—her own strange, sweet beauty. She is irresistible, Walter. You remember that Englishman who stayed over at the Cranstons'? Well, you know what a connoisseur of beauty every one thought him. You ought to have heard him after he had seen Numè. He was simply wild about her—called her a dainty piece of Dresden china—a rose and lily and cherry blossom in one."

"Did he tell Numè so?"

"No, he didn't get the chance. He made the *awful* blunder of telling her father so. *He* (Mr. Watanabe) disagreed very politely with him—said his daughter was augustly homely, and wouldn't let the poor little thing out of his sight for a month after. Really, Walter, you needn't chuckle over it,—for Numè suffered dreadfully about it. If you won't laugh I'll tell you what she said to me afterwards, though I believe it was you, yourself, you wretch, who taught her the words. I told her how sorry I was that the Englishman had been so stupid; because she had told us never to praise her to her father—and at any rate not to let any gentleman do so. Well, I half apologized to her, because, you know, I had taken him to their house, and she said, 'Numè not lig' Egirisu' (Englishman)—'he cot-tam.' I *know* she did not know what the word meant, poor little thing, and I spent half a day explaining to her *why* it was not proper to use such an expression. Yes, you can laugh—you wicked thing—but really, Walter, I won't let that child listen to you any longer."

Mrs. Davis left her husband almost in convulsions over this, and stole on tiptoe to the girl's room. She was sleeping without a pillow under her head. Beside her on the bed was a small English-Japanese dictionary. Mrs. Davis picked it up and glanced at a page which was turned over. It was a page of the letter J. Towards the bottom of the page was the word "jolly," with the interpretation, "to be merry—gay."

Her husband's definition had been unsatisfactory to Numè, and she had looked it up in her little dictionary.

XVII

"Still a Child"

The next day Numè seemed strangely loath to return home. For eight long years the girl had thought almost constantly of Orito and their marriage which had always seemed so far away. Now that he had come home, and the marriage seemed but a matter of a few weeks, she was seized with a sudden fear and dread of she knew not what. Long after she had finished breakfast she still lingered with the Davises, and though once or twice she had gone restlessly to the door and looked out across the fields toward where her own home was, she seemed in no hurry to leave. Finally Mrs. Davis had spoken to her, and asked if she did not think they would be expecting her. Numè clung to the American lady's hands with a sudden terror.

"Numè is *still* nerviss," she said.

"Shall I go back with you, dear?"

"No; *let* me stay with you."

About eleven in the morning, however, Orito walked through the rice fields and came himself to bring her home. Mrs. Davis saw him alone first, and after they had exchanged greetings and talked for a time of their mutual friends in America, she told him of the girl's agitation and how, at the last moment, she had broken down. The young man appeared to be very much concerned, and begged Mrs. Davis to tell Numè that she had nothing whatever to fear from meeting him. So Mrs. Davis went into the next room to fetch Numè. She put her arm round the girl and drew her gently into the room where Orito was. Numè did not raise her eyes to look at him. He, on the other hand, looked at her very keenly, taking note of every sweet outline of her face and form. To please his father he had resumed the Japanese costume, and now, dressed in his hakama, he looked every inch a Japanese gentleman, and should not have alarmed Numè so seriously. Yet his manners had lost some of the old Japanese polish, and as he crossed to her side and lifted her little hand to his lips, it seemed more the act of a foreigner than that of a Japanese.

At the light touch of his lips on her hand Numè's confidence returned. She smiled, shyly, at him. Orito was the first to speak.

"You are not much changed, Numè," he said. "You look just as I expected you would—and—and you are still a child."

Numè opened her little fan, and then closed it with a swing.

"And you, I thing you so changed that you must be Americazan," she said, shyly.

They sat and talked very politely to each other for some time, neither of them alluding to their proposed marriage; in fact, both of them seemed anxious to steer away from the subject altogether. Orito addressed her in Japanese, but she, with a strange wish to show off to him her pitifully limited knowledge of the language of which she was extremely proud, answered him in English.

Mrs. Davis drew Numè into the next room, before she left, and raising her little flushed face, looked down into her eyes as though she would fain have discovered what was going on in her little heart.

"Are you disappointed, dear?"

"No; *me*?—I am *vaery* joyous," the girl answered, candidly.

XVIII

The Meeting

How different was the meeting between Cleo Ballard and Arthur Sinclair! He had traveled over night from Kyoto, and because there were no sleeping accommodations on the train he had passed a very uncomfortable night. Consequently, when he arrived in Tokyo the next morning he was in anything but a happy frame of mind. He had gone directly to the hotel, and had followed his card to the Ballards' suite of rooms. Mrs. Ballard was ill, as usual. Tom had gone out, and Cleo was waiting alone for him. She had slept very little through the night, and there were dark shadows under her eyes. She had stayed awake thinking of Sinclair, and of his unkindness in failing to meet them. One moment she thought of him bitterly, and of his seeming indifference to her, the next her mind was thrilled with the wonder and tenderness of her love, which lost sight of his every fault. And now his little card lay in her hand, and her heart was beating to suffocation, for the footsteps that she knew so well, the tall, athletic figure, and the deep voice she had learned to adore. She had tried to steel herself for this meeting, telling herself that she ought to punish him for failing to meet her, but as his tall figure loomed up beside her she forgot everything save that she loved him—loved him better than all else on earth, that she had come thousands of miles to be with him, and that she would never leave him again. For a moment neither of them spoke. They looked at each other, the one with hungry, yearning love, the other with keen scrutiny, together with an honest endeavor to call up some of the old passion he had once had for her.

The girl's voice was almost frantic:—

"Why don't you speak to me, Arthur;—have you ceased to—to love me?"

"Why of—of course not, Cleo."

She went close to him and put her hands on his shoulder, looking into his fine, fair face with beseeching, beautiful eyes. What man could have resisted her, whether he loved her or not? Sinclair's arms closed about her, and somewhat of the old passion did return as he kissed her, and held her there. But she had broken down, and was sobbing pitifully, hysterically, in his arms.

"Why, Cleo, what is the matter, dear?"

He drew her to a small lounge and sat down with her, putting his arm affectionately about her, and drawing her close to him.

"Oh, I don't know," she sobbed; "but I—I—Oh, Arthur, I thought all sorts of awful things about you. That you—that you did not love me—that you did not want me to come—and—and—but I know it is not true, now—and you will forgive me?"

She waited for his denial, almost longing to hear him reprove her because her fears were unfounded. Instead, he merely kissed her, saying she was a foolish little girl.

After Cleo had quieted down a little she began to tell him of different home matters which she thought would interest him; but after listening for a while to his monosyllabic answers she stopped talking and turned her head away with the old pique and distrust. The distrust or pain of one we love very dearly cuts like a knife and wrings the heart, but where we do not love it irritates. It had always been so with Sinclair. When, during their engagement in America, the girl had shown resentment or anger against him for any cause, it had always had the effect of making him nervous, sometimes almost unkind. On the other hand, when she had put her entire trust in him, believed in and loved him unquestioningly, he seldom could find the heart to undeceive her. Now, as he looked at her pained, averted face, he felt only a vague weariness, almost a dislike for her. There was a touch of impatience in his voice: "What is the matter now, Cleo?"

"Nothing," the girl answered, proudly. "Only I thought perhaps you'd rather not hear me talk. You do not answer when I ask you anything, and I don't think you even hear what I say."

"Don't let us quarrel already, Cleo."

The girl melted. "No!" she said; and her feelings choked her.

"How is your mother?" he asked, mechanically.

She rose from beside him. "Come and see mother, Arthur. She is not at all well, and was quite put out about your not meeting us."

They passed into the mother's room together, and Sinclair was soon forced to listen to the querulous reproaches of the invalid.

XIX

CONFIDENCES

A few days later the Davises, together with several other Americans, swooped down, en masse, on Cleo, and she soon found herself surrounded by old acquaintances and friends. Mrs. Davis had heard of her arrival from Takashima, and had come to her at once. The two friends had so much to say to each other that Cleo was in a happy frame of mind. Sinclair had spent the former day entirely with her, and had been as tender and thoughtful as of old. After the first constraint had worn off and they had grown more used to each other, and the man had settled the matter with himself that she was the woman with whom he was to spend the rest of his life, he had called up all the gentleness and tenderness he could summon. If it was a poor substitute for love, it was, nevertheless, more welcome to the hungry heart of the girl than the indifference she had fancied she had detected, and which she now told herself was imaginary.

"My dear," said Mrs. Davis, "you *must* come and spend a few days with me at my house. I have such a pretty place—quite a little way from the city, and in the most charming spot imaginable. The house is large enough, almost, to be one of our own. I had wings built onto it after I had been there awhile, and really, it is so much more comfortable and homelike than the hotel."

"Indeed, I will come," Cleo answered. "Jenny—I want to see everything there is to see here. You know Arthur likes the country, and has an idea he'd like to settle here altogether. He says, however, it depends on me—and I want to see lots of the place before I decide. I do hope I will like it, for his sake."

"You certainly will get to like it."

"Yes, but I'm afraid I shall get lonely for America and Americans."

"No, you won't, Cleo, because there are scores of Americans here, to say nothing of tourists from all over Europe. In fact, I intend giving a big party in your honor, my dear. We haven't had one here for—oh, for ages! We could invite all the Japanese we know, and all the Americans and English worth knowing."

So the two friends chatted on, turning from one subject to another. At one time they had been almost inseparable, and confided in each other on all subjects. Hence, it was not surprising that Mrs. Davis, with characteristic familiarity and bon-camaraderie, should dash into the subject of Cleo's marriage.

"When is it to be, my dear?" she asked. "Sinclair is a splendid catch. Every one thinks worlds of him here, and—well, he is charming as far as his own personality goes."

Cleo was silent a moment. Then she said, abruptly: "Jenny, sometimes I fear that Arthur does not actually love me. I do not know why I should think so. He is always so kind to me. I suppose I am foolish."

"Of course you are. Why, Cleo, it would be—a—a perfect tragedy if he did not—it would be dreadful."

The girl sighed. Her words were halting, for she hesitated to ask even her closest friend such a question: "Does he—has he paid any one *here* much—a—attention?"

"No, indeed. He doesn't *like* Japanese women much—he told me so himself. Says they are all alike. That they haven't any heart."

"Is it true?"

"Well, dear, I don't know. It is not true of all of them, at any rate. There is one girl I know who is the dearest, best-hearted little thing in the world. Cleo, she is the sweetest thing you ever saw. I won't attempt to describe her to you, because I am not a poet, and it would take a poet to describe Numè."

"Numè?"

"Yes—Mr. Takashima's little sweetheart, you know. Ever heard him speak of her?"

Cleo Ballard had become suddenly very still and quiet. The other woman rattled on, without waiting for an answer.

"She has waited for him eight years, and—and I actually believe she still loves him. She seems to take it as a matter of course that she loves him, and doesn't see anything strange at all in her doing so, in spite of the fact that she was just a little girl when he went away." She paused a moment, smiling thoughtfully. "Really, Cleo, it is the prettiest thing in the world to see them together. He is rather stiff and formal, but just as gentle and polite as anything, and she, poor little creature, thinks he is the finest thing alive."

Cleo Ballard caught her breath with a sudden pain. She had grown quite white. "Jenny, don't let's talk of—of the Japanese now. I—I—don't care for them much."

"Don't *care* for them! Why, you *must* get over any feeling like that if you intend living here. However, even if you dislike every Japanese in

Japan, you'd change your mind, perhaps, after you knew Numè. You really ought to see her—she—why, my dear, what is the matter? You look quite faint."

"Oh, it is nothing, dear; only don't talk about this—this girl—really, I—I feel as though I shouldn't like her, and I am sure she won't like me."

"Oh, come now; you're not well, that's all. Here, sit down. You are tired after the long trip."

She left the girl's side to go over to Tom and Sinclair, who were talking over old college days. Cleo heard her praising her new protégé. Sinclair looked a trifle bored, though Tom was interested.

"Yes, they are all pretty, more or less," Sinclair said, languidly; "but the deuce is, they are too much alike."

"Well, Numè *is* different. Really, Mr. Sinclair, I am surprised you have not met her. But you will all see her at my party. You know we're going to have one for Cleo at my house," she added.

XX

Sinclair's Indifference

When Mrs. Davis had said Sinclair did not care for Japanese women she had merely spoken the truth. With the unreasoning prejudice of a westerner, he had taken a dislike to them, hardly knowing himself why he did so. Perhaps one of the reasons lay in the fact that when he had come to Japan he had been too acutely aware of his engagement, and that his wife would likely make her home there in Japan. For this reason he avoided the distractions that the tea-houses offered to most foreigners, going there only occasionally with parties of friends; but, unlike most western men, who generally consider it their privilege when in Japan to be as lawless as they desire, he had got into no entanglements whatever. That he had been called upon constantly, as consul, to help various Americans out of such scrapes with Japanese women, had made him more prejudiced against them.

On the night of Mrs. Davis' party, he stood in a doorway looking on at the gayly mixed throng. Here were Americans, English, French, Germans, and a good sprinkling of the better class Japanese. Mrs. Davis' house was entirely surrounded by balconies, which she had had specially built in American fashion, and the guests wandered in and out of the ball-room on to these balconies, or down into the gayly lighted garden; under the shadows of the trees, illumined, in spots only, by the flaring light of hundreds of Japanese lanterns, scattered like twinkling swinging lamps all through the gardens, and on the lawn. Cleo Ballard was looking very beautiful; and because she was undoubtedly the prettiest woman in the room she was surrounded the entire evening. Sinclair had once told her laughingly that he gave her carte blanche to flirt all she desired. In his secret heart, like most men, he was opposed to this pastime (for women). Not that he was entirely free from it himself. By no means; but sometimes the ring of falsity and untruth in it all struck the finer sense of the man. Perhaps he was a trifle bored that night. He watched wearily the dancers passing back and forth, the filmy laces and beautiful summer gowns; and he sighed. Somehow, he was not a part of the scene, for with the peculiarity of a traveler, Sinclair detested anything smacking of conventionality, and most parties (in society) are formal to a great degree—at least on the surface. Quite late in the evening Mrs. Davis, who had disappeared for a time from the ball-room, returned, bringing with her a young girl. Sinclair could not see her face at first, because her head was turned from him. She was dressed very simply in a soft white gown, cut low at the neck, the sleeves short to the elbows. She wore no jewels whatever, but in the mass of dense black hair, braided carelessly and coiled just above the nape of her neck, were a few red roses. Something in the girlish poise of the figure, the slim, unstudied grace of the neck, and rounded arms, caused Sinclair to move deliberately from his position by the door, and pass in front of her. Then he saw her face. There was something piteous in the girl's expression. He could not have told what there was in her face that struck him so with the peculiarity of its beauty. Her nationality puzzled him. As the guests began to crowd about her, the girl lost her repose of manner. She looked frightened and troubled. With a few quick strides, Sinclair was beside Mrs. Davis, waiting to be introduced. Almost as in a dream he heard his hostess say, half jokingly:

"Numè, I am going to introduce you to a—a hater of Japanese woman—he is our consul, Mr. Sinclair. You *must* cure him, my dear," she added; and then smiling at Sinclair she said: "Arthur, *this* is Numè, Miss Watanabe, of whom I told you."

The girl raised her little oval face, and looked very seriously at him. She held her hand out; she had learned from the Americans the habit of shaking hands. Sinclair felt a strange, indescribable sensation as her little hand rested in his; it was as if he held in his hand a little trembling, frightened wild bird.

XXI

"Me? I Lig' You"

For a moment Sinclair was at a loss what to say to Numè, and as she had not spoken he did not know whether she understood the English language or must be addressed in Japanese.

"Will you not let me get you a seat somewhere where there is not such a crowd?" he asked, speaking in English.

"Ess," she answered, looking almost helplessly at him, as Mrs. Davis came towards them with a fresh company of Americans, all eager to meet her. Numè belonged to the Kazoku order of Japanese (the nobles), the most exclusive class in Japan. They lived, as a rule, in the Province of Kyushu, and their women were supposed to be extremely beautiful, and kept in great seclusion, as the daughters of nobles usually are. Numè's father, however, had gone into business in Tokyo, and later had become a large land-owner there, so that the girl had mingled very little with her own class.

"I am going to take Miss Watanabe somewhere where she can breathe," Sinclair said to Mrs. Davis, and added: "Don't bring any more along just now. I judge by her face she is scared to death already."

The girl looked gratefully at him. "Ess, I nod lig' big crowd *joyful* ladies and gentlemen," she said, haltingly.

He found a couple of seats close by a window, where a soft breeze came through, and fanned her flushed little face. In spite of what Mrs. Davis had told her of Sinclair's not liking Japanese girls, with the usual confidence of a little woman in a tall man, Numè felt protected from the curious crowd when with him. She told him so with a shy artlessness that astonished him.

"Me? I lig' you," she said, shyly. "You are *big*—and thad you nod lig' poor liddle Japanese womans—still I lig' you jus' same."

"I like some of them," he said, lamely, confounded by the girl's direct words. "You see, I have not met any Japanese *ladies*, and the Japanese girls I have met always struck me as being—well, er—too gay to have much heart."

Numè shook her head. "Japanese girl have big, big heart," she said, making a motion with her hands. "Japanese boy go long way from home—see all the big world; bud liddle Japanese girl stay at home with fadder and mudder, an' vaery, vaery good, *bud* parents luf *always* the boy. Sometimes Japanese girl is *vaery* sad. Then account she stay at home *too* much, but she not show that she is vaery sad. She laugh and talk so thad the parents do nod see she is vaery sad."

Sinclair did not interrupt her. Her odd way of telling anything was so pretty and her speech so broken that he liked better to hear her talk. But the girl stopped short here, and looked quite embarrassed a moment. Then she said:

"Numè talk too much, perhaps?" Her voice was raised questioningly.

"No—no—Miss Numè cannot talk too much."

"Oa," the girl continued, smiling saucily, "Americazan girl talk too much also?"

"Sometimes."

"That you do not lig' liddle Japanese girl—do you lig' Americazan big proud girl?"

"No"—smiling. "Do you like the big proud American girl, Miss Numè?"

"Ess," she answered, half doubtingly. "Americazan lady is *vaery* pretty. Sometimes she has *great big heart*—*then* she change, and she is liddle, liddle heart—*vaery* mean woman."

"What makes you say that?"

"Oh! Numè watch everything," the girl answered, shrewdly.

Sinclair stayed by Numè's side almost the entire evening. She did not know how to dance; he did not care to; and as she told him quite candidly that she liked him to sit with her better than any one else in the room, he needed no further excuse. The girl's beauty and naivete captivated him, and in spite of her artlessness there were so many genuine touches of shrewdness and cleverness about her. Sinclair was converted into the belief that Japanese women were the most charming women he had met—at least, if the ladies were all as sweet and pretty as Numè.

During the evening Cleo Ballard paused in a dance, close by them. She had noticed the attention Sinclair had paid the girl from the beginning. He did not see her at first, but was looking with almost fascinated eyes into the strangely interesting face of the Japanese maiden. Sinclair had not once danced with Cleo through the entire evening, nor had he been by her side even. He had told her he did not like dancing, and on this plea had left her to the throngs of admirers who surrounded her, eager for a dance. There was a look of bitter pride on Cleo's face as she looked at him. In America Sinclair had always made it a point to attach himself almost scrupulously to her, and although she had always felt something lacking in his love for her, it pleased her that at least he had never given her cause to be jealous of any other women. Her voice sounded harsh even to her own ears.

"Perhaps, Arthur, you will introduce me—to—to your friend?" she said.

The same pique that always irritated him so was in her voice now. It was, he told himself, the reminder to him of his bondage; for long ere this the man had admitted to himself that he did not love her. He was too staunch by nature, however, knowing her love for him, to break with her. He rose stiffly from his seat beside Numè, his face rather flushed.

"Certainly," he said, coldly, and pronounced the two girls' names.

Instinctively the woman nature in Numè scented a rival—possibly an enemy. She wished the American gentleman would sit down again. She could not understand why he should stand just because the beautiful shining American lady had wanted to know her. The American girl's partner tapped her lightly on the shoulder, reminding her of the dance, and once more she glided away, leaving a vague unrest behind.

"Is the beautiful Americazan lady your betrothed?"

The man started, though he evaded the question.

"What makes you ask that?"

"All of us have betrothed," the girl said, vaguely. "See, I will show you *my* betrothed. He stands over there now—talking to the same pretty Americazan lady."

"Takashima!" said Sinclair.

"Ess," the girl answered, happily.

Takashima was talking very seriously to Cleo Ballard. There was an impatient, almost pettish, look on her face. She seemed anxious to get away from him. Sinclair saw her make a motion to Mrs. Davis, and in some way the two women managed to get rid of the Japanese. They stood talking for a moment together, and Sinclair saw them look over in his direction. He noted Cleo's movements almost mechanically, his mind being more absorbed in what Numè had told him about her betrothal to Takashima.

"When does the wedding take place?" he asked, abruptly.

"Oh! I not know. *We*—Orito and *me*—do *not* like much to hurry, the fadders make great haste," she said.

Sinclair looked down at her thoughtfully, studying her with a strange pang at his heart.

"So you are Takashima's little sweetheart," he said, slowly. "He used to tell us about you in America. He said you were the prettiest thing on earth, and the boys didn't believe him, of course, but, after all—he spoke only the truth."

Again the girl smiled.

"When I was liddle, liddle girl," she said, "Orito carry me high way up on his shoulder. Now I grow big and polite, and he is that far away to me, and I thing' we are strangers."

The man was silent. "But I am *vaery* happy," she continued, "because some day I will be altogether with Orito, then we will be much luf for each other again."

"May you always be happy, little woman," Sinclair said, almost huskily. "Happiness is a priceless treasure; we throw away our chances of it sometimes recklessly, for a joy of a moment only."

Mrs. Davis' voice broke in on them. She looked quite coldly at Sinclair.

"Come, Numè," she said, "I want you to meet some other people."

XXII

ADVICE

Mrs. Davis drew Numè into a corner of the balcony, and sat down to give her a little lecture.

"Now, dear, I'm going to speak to you, not as your hostess, but as your—a—chaperon—and friend. You must not speak too familiarly to any man. Now, you ought not to have sat with Mr. Sinclair so long. There were lots of other men around you, and you didn't speak to any of them."

"Bud I do *nod* lig' all the udder mans," the girl protested. "*Me?* I lig' only the—a—Mister Sinka."

"Yes; but, Numè, you must not like people so—so quickly. And you must not let any one know it, if you do."

"Oa, I tell him so," the girl said, stubbornly. "I tell Mr.—Sinka thad I lig' him *vaery* much; and I ask thad he sit with me, so thad too many peoples nod to speak to me."

Mrs. Davis looked very much concerned at this confession.

"Now, that *was* imprudent, my dear; besides, you know," she spoke very slowly and deliberately, "Mr. Sinclair is to be married soon to Miss Ballard, and so you ought to be very particular, so that no one can have the chance to say anything about you."

The girl's bright eyes flashed.

"Mr. Sinka nod led me thing' thad," she said, remembering how Sinclair had evaded the question. "I ask him thad the pretty lady is betrothed and he make me thing'—no."

Mrs. Davis was silent a moment.

"Er—that's only a way American men have, Numè. You must not believe them; and be very careful not to tell them you like them—because—because they—they often laugh at girls who do that."

Numè did not stir. She sat very still and quiet.

Mr. Davis joined them, and noticing the girl's constrained face, he inquired what was the matter.

"Nothing at all, my dear," the American lady said. "I was just giving Numè some pointers."

"Look here, Jenny, you'll spoil her—make her into a little prig, first thing you know. At least, she is genuine now, and unaffected."

"Walter," Mrs. Davis said, rising with dignity, "Mrs. Ballard thought it outrageous for Sinclair to have sat with her all evening. I never knew him to do such a thing before with any one. That makes it all the more noticeable. Cleo, too, was quite perturbed."

When the party broke up and the guests were slowly passing into their jinrikishas, numbers of them lingered in the garden, bidding laughing farewells.

Numè, who was spending the night with Mrs. Davis, stood a lonely little figure in the shadow of the balcony. She did not wish to say good-bye to any of them—she did not like the pretty Americans, she told herself, because she did not believe them any longer.

Sinclair went up to her, holding out his hand.

"Good-night, Miss Numè," he said.

The girl put her little hand behind her.

"Numè not lig' any longer big Americazan gentlemans," she said. "Mrs. Davees tell me nod to lig'—goonight,"—this last very stiffly and politely.

The man smiled grimly: "Ah, Miss Numè," he said, "you must always choose your own—like whom you choose;—don't let any one tell you who to like and who not to."

He looked searchingly at her face a moment, then turned and passed out with the other guests, understanding the truth.

XXIII

AFRAID TO ANSWER

It was over ten days since the Ballards had arrived in Tokyo. Still Cleo had not given Takashima the promised answer. It was not that she any longer hesitated for the sake of any sentiment she might have had for him, which was the case on the steamer, but that, having led him on to believe in her, she had not the courage to let him know the truth. Moreover, there was a certain assured, determined look always about his face which frightened her. Cleo was a coward if she was anything. It would have been a relief to her to have confided in Mrs. Davis, and perhaps to have her break the truth to him, as gently as possible; but knowing of her strong affection for Numè her heart misgave her whenever she thought of doing so, and she dreaded the contempt, perhaps anger, that such a revelation would cause in Mrs. Davis. So she put off from day to day. Whenever Takashima called on her at the hotel she was either out, or one of a party, so that he found no chance whatever of speaking to her alone. The girl did everything in her power to avoid being alone with him. If the young man guessed anything of the truth, he never showed it, for he was persistent in his visits, and when he did get a chance to speak to Cleo would talk to her as naturally and confidently as he had done those last days on the boat. It terrified Cleo that he refused to be discouraged, that in spite of the almost direct way in which she at times ignored him, he let her understand, in every conceivable way in his power, that he had not lost faith in her, letting her believe that he understood that she, having so many friends, must necessarily be surrounded for the first few days, at least. Cleo did not know whether he had heard of her engagement to Sinclair or not. If he had heard of it he simply ignored it, putting it behind him as so much gossip, and as an impossibility, seeing the girl had told him nothing of it herself, and had almost deliberately encouraged him to believe that his own suit was not in vain. It was no use for her to try before Takashima to let him see that she and Sinclair were more to each other than friends, because Sinclair was no aid to her in the matter. He had become strangely cold and reticent, and though he was always the essence of politeness and attention to her, still he might have been just so to any woman friend.

Meanwhile, Takashima had not once reminded her of her promise to answer him. He told himself he could afford to wait now that he was so sure of her; besides, his mind was a good deal absorbed in going over the old familiar haunts of his boyhood, and trying in every way possible to do little acts to please his father, and which would make up for the long years of separation. With Numè he was on the best of terms, they being, however, more as brother and sister or very dear friends, rather than lovers; for Numè had become as anxious as he to put the marriage off for a time, and the subject was seldom broached between them, though their fathers often alluded to it, and urged haste.

Although Takashima and Sinclair were excellent friends, neither of them had ever mentioned Cleo Ballard's name to the other. Sinclair knew nothing whatever of Takashima's love for the girl, or that there had been anything between them; for both Tom and Cleo had been very careful to avoid telling him, knowing Takashima to be an old friend of his. Besides, perhaps Sinclair's interest in her had flagged, so that, in spite of her beauty and vivacity, his engagement began to pall on him. It galled him beyond measure that he did not have the freedom to go and come when he pleased. This was another reason why he avoided, whenever it was possible, talking about the girl, not wishing to be reminded of her when it was unnecessary; for an engagement where there is no love is the most irksome of things.

So they talked, instead, of Numè. Sinclair was intensely interested in her. He had a half-pleasant, half-painful memory of her angry eyes and flushed face when she had refused to shake hands with him in parting that night of the party. He had not seen her since then, though he had paid several visits to Mrs. Davis, and even to Takashima's home. Orito told him she had taken an unaccountable whim, after the party, to become very strict in Japanese etiquette, and that since then she had been living in great seclusion, not even he (Orito) seeing her, save in the presence of her father. And in these talks about Numè, with her betrothed, Sinclair made one discovery which astonished, and strange to say, pleased him—it was that Takashima did not love her—and further, that the girl did not actually love Takashima, though they were the best of friends. He wondered what understanding they had come to on the subject, and whether they had bluntly told each other that they did not love each other.

XXIV

Visiting the Tea Houses

Quite a large party of Americans, which included the Ballards, Sinclair, the Davises, the Cranstons, Fannie Morton, and others, visited the picturesque tea-houses on the highway between Yedo (Tokyo) and Kyoto. The oddly-built houses, with their slanting roofs, the beauty of their gardens, the perfume-scented air, rich with the odor of cherry and plum blossom, all contributed to lend an air of delight and sunshine to the visits, and the Americans watched with pleasure and interest the pretty waitresses and geisha girls, who seemed a part of the scene, as they tripped back and forth before them in their brightly-colored kimonas, played on the samisen and koto (harp), or danced for them.

One girl with an unusually pretty round face, and bright, sly eyes, attracted especial attention. She waited on Cleo and Tom Ballard, kneeling on the ground in front of them, holding a small tray, while they drank the tiny cups of hot sakè. Cleo did not like the taste of sakè. She told the little waitress so, who, although not understanding a word the American girl had said, nodded her head knowingly, and brought tea for her instead. She tripped on her little heels across the floor, padded about three feet with rice straw, looking back over her shoulder to smile at Tom, to the amusement of that gentleman, and the irritation of some of the American ladies.

"Japanese girls are—rather bold," Rose Cranston said, sharply.

"They are—all right," Tom answered, ready to defend them.

"Yes," said Fanny Morton, with her usual cynicism. "Naturally you think so. Perhaps we women would, too, if she peeped at us out of her wicked little eyes as she does at you."

Cleo Ballard laughed, a slow, aggravating, silvery laugh.

"I think they are charming, Miss Morton," and then to Tom, "they are too funny, Tom. It is the cutest thing in the world to see the way in which they deliberately ignore us poor—females. At least they don't make any pretense of liking us, as we would do in America."

The little geisha girl had come near them again, with a couple of others. Thy were all pretty, with a cherry-lipped, peepy-eyed, cunning prettiness. They stood in a group together, their fans in their hands, glancing smilingly at the American men, undisguisedly trying to flirt with them.

Rose Cranston, thoroughly disgusted, said loftily: "Nasty little things, these Japanese women are."

"Not at all," said Tom, and went over to them, followed by Cleo and Sinclair.

"What is your name, little *geesa* girl?" Cleo asked, a touch of patronage in her voice. The three girls looked at each other and giggled. Sinclair looked amused. He put the question to them in Japanese, and they answered him readily: "Koto, Kirishima, and Matsu."

"What very pretty names!" the American girl said, graciously. "Er—do you dance, as well as—as serve tea?"

Again the girls laughed, and Sinclair told them what the American lady had said. The girls nodded their heads brightly, and a few minutes after were dancing for the Americans.

"Do they make much money?" Cleo asked Takashima, who had joined them.

"Yes, but they spend a great deal on their clothes. They are very gay."

"Yes, they seem so," Cleo said, thoughtfully, "and yet somehow they look kind of tired and fagged out at times. I have been watching them quite closely, and noticed this about them in spite of the big show of gayety they affect."

"Their chief duty is to arouse mirth," the Japanese answered. "Therefore they must always appear joyful themselves. Some are very witty and accomplished, and if you understood Japanese, as you will some day, you would find a great deal to laugh at in what they say."

Towards evening the gardens began to fill up with more guests, and the geisha girls soon had their hands full. They talked and laughed with their guests, sang, danced, flirted, and played on odd musical instruments.

The geisha's chief attractions lie in her exquisite taste in arranging her hair, and in the beauty of her dress, the harmonious colors of which blend, according to a Japanese idea, in an unsurpassed way. Her manners, too, are very graceful, though the younger geishas are inclined to be boisterous, and laugh perhaps too much. Moreover, the situations of their houses and the picturesqueness of their tea gardens lend an air of enchantment and charm to the geisha girl and her surroundings. Although the geisha has little history, having first come into existence the middle of last century, her popularity is such in Japan that no parties are thought to be complete without her presence to brighten it up,—to entertain the guests with her accomplishments and infectious mirth, and to dance and play for them. Although her life is essentially rapid and gay, yet, in spite of her lapses from virtue at times, the geisha always retains her native modesty and grace. It is true, many of them are extremely familiar with foreigners, who are their best patrons; yet, in spite of this, the more modest and virtuous a geisha is the more are her services required.

The remnant of the old Samourai class of Japanese, although very taciturn and grave in deportment, are, nevertheless, extremely fond of the distractions offered by the tea-houses. They are addicted to such pleasures. The snow, the full moon, flowers of every season, national and local fêtes,— these all serve as pretexts for forming convivial parties which meet in the picturesque tea-houses and drink the sakè hot, in tiny cups, twenty or more to the pint. The fact that they are so much sought after, however, has not spoiled the geisha girl. In fact, when you have become acquainted with any one of them, you soon discover that she is quite diffident, modest, and gentle.

There are a great many tea-houses scattered over Tokyo, and on the highway between that city and Kyoto; and it is notable that the style of dress of the waitress and the geisha, as well as the dancing and other amusements, very distinctly differ from each other in each locality. Hence, one who starts out in the morning and visits a number of different tea and geisha gardens is hardly likely to be bored, as he will find new attractions in each place.

XXV

SHATTERED HOPES

It was in the month of April that Orito had arrived home—April, the month of cherry blossoms, the month when the devout Japanese celebrate the birth of the great Buddha. On the eighth of that month devotees go to the temples where the ceremony is performed. It consists simply of pouring tea over the sacred image. They also make trifling contributions to the temple, carrying home with them some of the tea, which is supposed to contain certain curative properties if administered to one suffering from disease. Of later years this religious ceremony has been practically done away with, although a few devout followers still observe it. Instead of performing any ceremony in memory of Buddha, many of the people commemorate the month of April by simply being very gentle, kind, loving, and happy among themselves during the month. It is at this time of year that the people stroll out for hanami (flower picnic), clad in fantastic costumes, some with masks over their eyes. To the foreigner the surging crowd of holiday makers will cause them to think of an endless masquerade. No one is allowed to pluck the cherry blossom during the entire month, and perhaps this is the reason that the flower grows so luxuriantly throughout the island, as it is not plucked by unscrupulous lovers who might have a special taste for it.

It was because of the fact that April is a month of peace and good-will to almost every one, when one puts off the cares of to-day until to-morrow, that Orito had failed to tell his parents of his love for the American girl. He had, instead, tried every means in his power to please the two old men, and would often sit by them for hours listening to their plans for his and Numè's future, without saying a word. Neither had he, as yet, spoken to Numè on the subject. That the girl was extremely fond of him he knew, but with the reasoning rather of an American than a Japanese he could not believe that she actually loved him, whom she really scarcely knew.

Over a month had passed by since his return home. One day in the month of May, when the fields were ablaze with a burning glory of azaleas, and the sun touched their wild crimson with dazzling splendor, Orito told his father and Omi of his love for the American girl. He had invited them both to go with him to Okubo, the western suburb of the capital, to see some new variety of the azalea; for with the birth of each new flower, every month, the Japanese celebrate fêtes in their honor. The noisy crowd of pleasure-seekers had driven them away from the scene, however, to a more secluded spot in the woods. Here Orito had told them, very gently but firmly, of his love for the beautiful American girl. The two old men remained perfectly silent, looking at each other with haggard, uncomprehending eyes. The dream of their life was shattered. There had not been a time since Numè was born that they had not talked joyously of the marriage of their two children, and in their strong pride in Orito they had sent him to America to become very learned and accomplished. It had seemed to them, sometimes, that the eight years never would come to an end. Now Orito had returned to them, but alas, how changed! He stood by them, slim and quiet, his face sad but determined, waiting for his father to speak.

Finally old Sachi rose to his feet.

"What does this mean?" he said, sharply. "Do you then wish to go against the command of your father? Must I then say I have lost my son?"

"No, father—I will be more your son than ever."

The old man's voice trembled.

"Duty!" he said, sternly. "That is the watchword for a Japanese. Did you forget that in America? Have you ceased to be Japanese?—duty first of all to your parents, to the wife and children to come, and last to yourself."

Orito was silent.

Omi now spoke. "Orito," he said, and his voice was quite dazed and stupid, "you really speak only in jest. Surely, it is now too late to change."

The young man's voice was very low:

"It would be too late had the marriage taken place—it is not too late now. Not so long as I have not ruined Numè's happiness as well as my own."

"Perhaps after you think this over you will change, my son," Sachi said, gently.

"Nay, father, I would rather see you reconciled. I cannot change in this. You do not understand. I love her with all my heart, and if—if she were impossible to me, I should surely die."

"Could you, then, leave your father to a comfortless, childless life?" the old man asked, sadly.

"We should go together," Orito said.

XXVI

Conscience

A pitiful constraint had settled over the households of Takashima Sachi and Watanabe Omi. The two old men saw each other not often now; for Sachi had not the strength to cross the eager vital will of his son, whom he loved so dearly, while Omi was too stunned and grieved to care to see them. So he and Numè remained in great seclusion for some days. Omi had as yet told Numè nothing of what Orito had told them. He was a shrewd old man, and there came to him a certain hope that perhaps the American girl would, after all, refuse to marry Orito. Consequently, he thought he would wait a while before telling the girl anything. Orito called on him each day with presents of tea and flowers, but each time the old man refused to see him, sending word that he and Numè were in retirement. This gave Orito no opportunity whatever of speaking to the girl alone. Sachi tried to convince him constantly that she actually loved him, and that it would be a cruelty now, not to marry her. The young man grew very despondent, though his resolve did not lose any of its firmness, Sachi had fallen into a pitiful dull apathy, taking interest in nothing about him, and refusing to take comfort from his son, who tried to be very devoted and kind to him. Often, too, he would upbraid Orito very bitterly. At such times the young man would leave the house and go out into the valleys and wander through the woodland paths, trying to forget his misfortunes in the beauty of his surroundings. He had not seen Cleo Ballard for some days, but he had written to her, telling her of what he had done. Cleo Ballard had read his letter with dread misgiving.

"Miss Cleo," it said very simply, "I have told my father and Mr. Watanabe that I cannot marry Numè-san because of my supreme love for you. I did not tell them last month, because it was the season of joy, and I wished to save them pain. Now they are very unhappy, but I tell myself that soon will you bring back joy to our house."

His assurance frightened her. She read the note over and over, as she sat before her dresser, her maid brushing her hair. She shook the hair from the maid's hands.

"I must be alone, Marie," she said, and the girl left her.

Long she sat in silence, no sound escaping her lips save one long trembling sigh of utter weariness and regret.

She looked at her image in the glass, seeing nothing of its beauty.

"You are a wicked woman, Cleo Ballard," she said, "a wicked, cruel woman, and—and—Oh! God help me—what shall I do?"

XXVII

Confession

Cleo Ballard did not answer Takashima's letter. All night long it rose up before her accusingly, and the next morning she dressed in feverish haste, and rushed off to her friend, Mrs. Davis.

"Jenny," she said, wildly, "I want to go away—I must go—I am stifling here. I must leave Tokyo—I—I—" she broke down and covered her face with her hands.

"Why, Cleo—what is it?" Her friend's kindly arms were around her.

"I can't tell you, Jenny. I can't tell you—you would hate me, and then, except Tom—Oh, Jenny, I can't afford now to lose any one's friendship."

"Nothing you can tell me, Cleo, would make me hate you. Is it some flirtation you have carried too far? Come, now, it used to relieve you to tell me all about these things in America. Who is it? Alliston? Cranston? or the Englishman?—or—or—"

"No—none of them—it—it—Oh, Jenny, I can't tell you."

"You must, Cleo—it will do you good, I know, and perhaps I can help you."

"It is—Takashima."

Jenny Davis' hands dropped from Cleo's shoulders.

"Orito!"

The two looked at each other in tragic silence.

"Cleo, how *could* you do it? There were enough without him;—when was it? how? tell me all about it—Oh! poor little Numè!"

"It was on the steamer—"

"On the steamer," her friend repeated, stupidly. "Yes, go on;—well, and what happened—you—?"

"Yes—I did it deliberately—I made him—care for me. I was lonely, and wanted to be amused. The passengers were uninteresting and stupid. He was different, with his gentle, odd ways. Sometimes I got almost frightened of myself, because he took everything so seriously. I did not mean to—to really hurt him. I wanted to see how a Japanese would act if he were in love, and—and Tom kept telling me how proof he was against women—and—Oh, Jenny, when he did speak out to me, I had not the courage, then, to tell him the truth. And all the time I knew it—but—"

Her friend's shocked face startled her.

"Yes; I understand," she said, bitterly. "I knew you would hate me—I deserve it—only I—"

Jenny Davis put her arms round her again.

"Dear, I don't hate you. Indeed, I don't, but it has startled me so. I am so—so shocked, because of Numè, and the two poor old men. I don't know what to say, but I'd stand by *you*, dear, against all the Japanese in Japan if it became necessary." She put her head against Cleo's, and the two friends wept in sympathy with each other, as women do.

"You must face the thing out, Cleo. Have you told Takashima yet?"

"No;—he sent me this to-day," she put the note despairingly into her friend's hands.

"How dreadful!—how perfectly awful!—you do not know the Japanese as I do, dear. It will just break the two old men's hearts. They have looked forward to his marriage with Numè all their lives. They don't love their children as we do in America. Their pride in them is too pathetic, Cleo; and when they disappoint them it is like a death-blow."

"Don't, Jenny—*don't*, please don't talk about them."

"But we must, Cleo. That is where the whole mistake has always been with you. You are too weak, Cleo. You can't look suffering in the face, and in consequence you do nothing to relieve it. Your duty is plain. Go right to Orito and tell him the truth."

"Jenny, I can't do it. He said once on the steamer that he would not scruple to take his life if he were very unhappy; and then he went on to tell me how common suicides were in Japan, and how the Japanese had not the smallest fear of death, and he seemed to think it would be a courageous act to—to take one's life. Jenny, I got so frightened that night I almost screamed out."

"But sooner or later you will have to tell him, Cleo. Don't let him know it solely by your marrying Sinclair. That would be too cruel;—tell him. Tell me, Cleo, do you think he actually believes you care for him?"

"Yes;—once I almost told him so—at least I led him to believe it— and it was true, almost, that night."

"Cleo!"

"You tell him, Jenny."

"I! Why, he wouldn't listen to me, Cleo."

Cleo got up desperately, and began pacing the floor.

"I will not give Arthur up, Jenny. You don't know how I love him—love him. I think day and night of him. I forgive him everything. He is cold often, and I am humiliated at his indifference at times, but I go on loving him better than ever. I can't help it;—I shall love him as long as I live."

Jenny Davis watched her with anxious eyes. She had known her for some years, had known her better qualities, her weaknesses, her strength; and her heart ached for her. She was so beautiful, with a lithe, grand, extraordinary beauty.

"Yes, Cleo," she said, slowly, "you are right. You must go away—right at once. There is a party of English tourists going to Matsushima Bay to-morrow. Pack a few things hastily and join them. I know them all well, and you know some of them, too."

"Yes," the girl agreed, eagerly. "And you *will* break it to him—you will save me—that—that pain."

"I will try, Cleo." The two women were silent a moment. Then Mrs. Davis said: "Cleo, does Arthur Sinclair know?"

Cleo's eyes were full of a vague terror "No—no—and he must not. Jenny, he is so strict about such things—he would despise me; and then, Mr. Takashima is his friend. He would not forgive me. Jenny, he *must* not know." After a time she said, almost wildly: "Jenny, I hate Takashima whenever I think of his alienating Arthur and me for even a moment, as he would do if—if Arthur found out."

XXVIII

JAPANESE PRIDE

The next day Cleo left Tokyo with the party of tourists. Takashima, who had called during the afternoon, found a note from her. It told him simply that she had decided to make a trip through the island, and as the party left that day she had no time save to write a hurried good-bye. The letter was weak, conventional in its phrases, and enigmatical. Had it been written to a westerner he would have understood at once; in fact, her manner, long before this, would have raised doubts as to her honesty toward him. It did not have that effect on Takashima, because it is the nature of the Japanese to believe thoroughly in one until they are completely undeceived. On returning home Orito found waiting for him a dainty note from Mrs. Davis, asking him to call on her.

It was a difficult task she had set herself—difficult even for a woman of Mrs. Davis' social and worldly experience.

When Orito looked at her with grave, attentive eyes, in which were no traces of distrust, she felt her heart begin to fail her before she had said a word. They talked of the weather, of the flowers, of the month, the foreigners in Tokyo, the pretty geisha girls—every subject save the one she had at heart. Finally she dashed into it all at once, almost desperately. Perhaps she had learned in that brief interview why it had been so hard for Cleo to tell him, for the young man's face was so earnest, pure, and true.

"Cleo has told me—I know all about that—and I—she told me to say—I mean—I know about your—your caring for her, and—"

The Japanese had risen sharply to his feet. He was deathly pale.

"Will madam kindly not speak of this?" he said. "I can only speak with Miss Ballard herself on this subject."

After he had left her Mrs. Davis sat down helplessly, and wrote a flurried letter to Cleo.

"Dearest Cleo," it ran, "I tried to tell him; tried harder than I ever tried to do anything in my life. But he would not let me speak—stopped me as soon as I got started, and I had not the heart to insist."

XXIX

Seclusion

Mrs. Davis had not seen Numè for some days. She had heard that the girl was living in strict seclusion, as it was customary for Japanese girls to do previous to their marriage. With a woman's quick wit and comprehension, however, Mrs. Davis understood that she had taken umbrage, and, perhaps, resented the lecture she had given her the night of the party. She was afraid, too, that in her earnest desire to serve both Cleo and Orito she had given Numè a false impression of Americans. Mrs. Davis was a good woman, and a wise one. She was determined that nothing on earth should prevent her friend's marriage with Sinclair. She knew Cleo Ballard well enough to know the wonderful goodness and generosity in her better nature. She knew also that she loved Sinclair with a love that should have been her salvation. In spite of all this, Mrs. Davis was genuinely fond of Numè, though not, of course, in the same way as she was of Cleo. It pained her, therefore, to think that Numè was probably suffering.

The day after Cleo left, she crossed the valley and went down to the house of Watanabe Omi. With her usual sang-froid, she asked to see Numè. Omi made some very polite apologies, saying his honorably unworthy daughter was entertaining a friend, and would the august American lady call the next day?

"No;" Mrs. Davis would like to see Numè's friend also; for Numè had told her she wanted her to meet all of them.

She passed into the girl's room with the familiarity of old acquaintance, for she and Numè had been great friends, and Omi thought so much of her that the American lady had got into the habit of coming and going into and out of his house just as she pleased, which was a great concession and compliment for any Japanese to make to a foreigner.

She found Numè sitting with another Japanese girl, playing Karutta. They laughed and talked as they played, and Numè seemed quite light-hearted and happy.

Mrs. Davis sat down on the mat beside her, and after having kissed her very affectionately, asked why she had not been over for so long.

"I come visite you to-morrow," the girl answered, looking a trifle ashamed, as Mrs. Davis regarded her reproachfully. Then, as she started to make further apologies, the American lady said, very sweetly: "Never mind, dear; I understand;—you did not like what I told you the other night."

Numè did not answer. The other Japanese girl watched Mrs. Davis curiously. Mrs. Davis turned smilingly to her and started to say something, but stopped short, a look of puzzled recognition on her face.

"I am sure I have seen your friend somewhere before, but I can't tell where," she said to Numè.

"Perhaps you seeing her at the tea garden, because Koto was, one time, geisha girl."

"Why, of course! I remember now. She was the pretty little Japanese girl who waited on us that day and made Rose Cranston so angry by flirting with Tom."

The girl was smiling at Mrs. Davis. She too recognized her. Mrs. Davis turned to Numè:

"I don't understand, Numè, how—how a geisha girl can be a friend of yours," she said.

Numè looked very grave.

"Japanese lady *always* have frien' who is also maid. Koto is my maid; also my frien'."

"I understand," the American lady said thoughtfully.

Japanese ladies usually treat their maids more as sisters than as maids. In fact, one of the duties of a maid is to act as companion to her mistress. Hence, it is necessary that the maid be quite accomplished and entertaining. Often a geisha girl will prefer to leave the tea-house where she is employed, to take a position as companion and maid to some kind and rich lady of the Kazoku and Samourai class, and in this way she learns to be very gentle and polite in her manners by copying her little mistress; besides, she will have a good home. It is a peculiar fact that Japanese holding positions such as maid, or, for a man, perhaps as retainer or valet, or even servant, become extremely devoted to their masters and mistresses, remaining with them until they are married, and sometimes preferring to remain with them after they have married, rather than marry themselves. It is no uncommon thing for them to make sacrifices, sometimes almost heroic ones, for their masters or mistresses.

XXX

Feminine Diplomacy

The next day Numè and Koto visited the American lady. Orito had gone up to Yokohama, Numè told her, and would not be back for several days.

"You will be very lonely then, dear."

Numè sat in her favorite position, on the floor at Mrs. Davis' knee. Koto trotted about the room, examining with extreme interest and curiosity the American furnishings and decorations.

"No; I nod be lonely," Numè said, "because I nod seen Orito *many* days—so I ged used."

"He must be a very bad boy to keep away from you so many days," Mrs. Davis said, playfully.

"Oh, no! Orito is *vaery good* boy." She sat still and thoughtful for a while, her feet drawn under her, her little hands clasped in her lap.

"Do the pretty Americazan ladies always luf when they marry?"

"Nearly always, Numè."

Numè nodded her head thoughtfully. "Japanese girls nod *always* luf," she said, wistfully. "Koto say only *geisha* girls marry for luf."

"That must be because they are thrown into contact with men and boys, while Japanese ladies are secluded. Is it not so, dear?"

"Ess. Mrs. Davees, do you lig' that I am goin' to marry Orito?"

"Yes, very much—I am sure you will be very happy with him. He is so good. No one has said anything to you about—about it, have they?" she added, anxiously, fearing perhaps the girl had heard of what Orito had told his father.

"No," she said. "No one talk of luf to Numè bud Mrs. Davees; thad is why Numè lig' to talk to you."

The American lady smiled.

"Suppose Japanese girl lig' instead some *nize, pretty* genleman, and she marry with some one she *nod* like?" She emphasized this question, and threw a charming glance at Mrs. Davis.

"Do you mean the case of a girl betrothed to one man and in love with another?"

"Ess."

"Why, I don't know what she could do then, Numè. What put such an idea into your head?"

Numè did not reply for a moment. Then she said, very shyly: "Numè *not* lig' the big, ugly Americazan genleman any more. I telling him so."

"Numè!"

"Ess, I tell Mr. Sinka I *nod* lig'—thad you telling me so."

"Well, Numè!" Mrs. Davis' voice betrayed her impatience. "What did you do that for?"

The girl half shrugged her little shoulders.

"Oa! I dunno."

"Numè, you *must* be careful how you speak to men. *Don't* tell them anything. If you like them, keep it to yourself; it's a good thing you told him you disliked him, this time, and did not leave him with the impression that you were in love with him. You know, dear, girls have to be very careful who they like."

"Bud, Mr. Sinka tell me nod to let *any one* choose for me—thad I lig'"—she paused a moment, and added vaguely, "thad I lig' who I lig'."

"Really, Numè, you might take my advice before Mr. Sinclair's," the older lady said, quite provoked.

XXXI

A Barbarian Dinner

The girls stayed to dinner with Mrs. Davis. Koto had never eaten an American dinner before, though Numè had grown quite used to it. Following the national custom, she ate all placed before her by her hostess, and Mrs. Davis, knowing of this little habit of hers, which was more an act of compliment to her hostess than of liking for the food, was always very careful not to serve her too much. She quite forgot that Koto would be altogether unused to the food. The two little Japanese women presented a very pretty contrast. Both were small and, in their way, pretty. Koto had a round-faced, bright-eyed, shy prettiness; while Numè's face was oval and pure in contour. She chatted very happily and confidently, now in Japanese to Koto, now in pretty broken English to Mr. and Mrs. Davis.

Koto ate her dinner in silence, her face strangely white and pitiful. Very bravely she ate the strange food, however, stopping at nothing. She looked with wonder at the butter (something the Japanese never use), puzzling for a moment what she was supposed to do with it, then picked the little round pat from the butter-plate, slipped it into her tea, and drank the tea.

Mr. Davis saw this act, and choked.

"What is the matter, Walter?"

"Er—er—hum—nothing, my dear! I—a—Oh, Lord!" This last exclamation was provoked by another act of Koto's. On the table was a small plate of chowchow. The servant passed it to Koto, thinking perhaps she would like some with her meat. Instead of helping herself to some, the girl held the dish in her hand, hesitated a moment, and then very heroically ate the hot stuff all up with the small china spoon in the dish. Her eyes were full of tears when she had finished.

"What is it, Koto-san?" Numè asked, gently.

"It is the barbarian food," the girl answered, desperately, in Japanese. "I do not like it."

Numè translated this to the Americans, apologizing for the remark by saying:

"Koto *always* been geisha girl. Tha's why she is nod *most* careful in her speech. It was *most* rude that she spik' so of the kind Americazan's food, *bud* the geisha girl is *only* stylish, and nod understan' to spik' polite to foreigners."

This elaborate, rather mixed apology, the Americans took very good-naturedly, telling Numè to assure Koto that they bore her no malice whatever, and that, in fact, they owed her an apology for not having remembered that she was a stranger to their food. Besides, the Americans were just as foolish when they had eaten Japanese food.

XXXII

The Philosophy of Love

After dinner Numè resumed her seat by Mrs. Davis, while her husband took Koto through the house, glad of an opportunity to air his limited knowledge of Japanese; for Numè seldom permitted them to address her save in English, pretending to make great fun of their Japanese in order to make them speak English to her. They, on the other hand, always praised her English extravagantly.

"I want you to promise me, Numè, that you will never tell any man you care for him again, unless it is Orito."

"Why shall I *promise*?" the girl asked.

"Because it is not the right thing to say to any one."

"But if I luf—"

"Nonsense; you are not going to love except as all good Japanese girls do—after your marriage."

"But you say one time thad is *shame* for me thad I only luf *after* I marry."

"Well, I have been thinking it over," the other answered, a trifle rattled—"and—and really, you are all so happy with things that way I wouldn't advise your changing the custom."

"Bud Japanese girl luf a *liddle* before they marry. After marriage big bit. Koto say geisha girl luf *big* bit *before* they marry. Koto luf vaery much Japanese boy in Tokyo—"

"That is good, and are they to be married?"

"Ah, no; because he worg *vaery* hard to mag' money, but Koto say mag' *vaery* liddle money, so she come worg' for me, and save—*afterward* they marry *vaery* habby."

Numè looked at the American lady with eyes full of wistful wondering: "I thing' I lig' vaery much thad I luf and be habby too. Numè nod know thad she luf Orito *vaery* much—Ess, she luf him *vaery* much, bud—sometimes I thing' I nod *luf* him *too* much; sometimes I thing' mebbe Orito nod luf *me* too much."

"Of course, you do love him, goosie. Now, don't begin thinking you don't, because one often convinces oneself of things that are not actually so."

"Bud I do *nod* thing' much of Orito," the girl contradicted; and added, shyly: "I thing', instead, of Mr. Sinka—but I not lig'—No! Numè nod lig' Mr. Sinka;" she shook her head violently.

Mrs. Davis called all the argument she could to her aid.

"You ought not to think of him, Numè; that is wicked, because he belongs to some one else."

The girl's face had lost its wistfulness. Now it was arch and complacent.

"Perhaps Numè is *vaery* wigged," she smiled. "Koto say all girls thad are habby are wigged."

"Koto is a bad girl if she told you that. Don't let her teach you about the geisha girls, dear—Er—every one knows they are not a good class, at all."

Numè tossed her head provokingly. "All the *same*, Numè still *thing'* of Mr. Sinka."

Her persistence astounded Mrs. Davis. She felt almost like shaking the girl; and yet there was something so sweet and innocent in her openly acknowledging that she thought of Sinclair.

She had not been out much, nor had she seen many people since the night of the party. Therefore, it was quite natural that, as Sinclair had made such an impression on her that night, she should think about him a great deal. Moreover, Koto, with a geisha girl's usual flippancy and love of anything savoring of romance, had perhaps fostered this feeling. The girls had discussed him.

Ever since he had told his father of his love for the American girl, Orito had been very kind to her, though sometimes Numè fancied he wished to tell her something. Her interest in Sinclair had not spoiled her loyalty to Orito, which she had felt and cultivated all these years. Koto had encouraged her in the idea of flirting with the American. That was all. She never for an instant thought of breaking off her betrothal with Orito. She had grown used to that, and, unlike Orito, she had not been in America, so that she still was Japanese enough to be obedient. Besides, she really did love Orito in a way that she herself did not comprehend. Because, although it pleased her very much to be with him, to chat and tell him all the news of the neighborhood in which they lived, ask his advice and opinion on different subjects, yet her mind kept constantly wandering from him, and she could call up no genuine warmth or enthusiasm in her affection for him. The truth was, her love for him was merely that of a young sister for a very dear brother, one from whom she had been parted for a long time.

XXXIII

What Can that "Luf" Be?

Perhaps Orito recognized this fact, and for that reason seldom wearied her with over-attention. He was tenderness itself to her; he took great interest in all her studies; played games with her and Koto; and tried in every way possible to make things pleasant for her. In this way a very dear sympathy had sprung up between them. Although Orito had told her nothing directly of his plans, yet he had often tried to give her some inkling of the state of affairs. Thus, he would say: "I will be your friend and brother forever, Numè-san."

Numè had a peculiar temperament for a Japanese girl. Although apparently open and ingenuous and artless in all things, nevertheless where she chose to be she could keep her own counsel, and one might almost have accused her of being sly. But then the girl was far from being as childish, or as innocent and contented, as she seemed at times. On the contrary, her nature was self-willed almost to stubbornness. She either loved one with all her strength, or she was indifferent, or she hated one fiercely. There was nothing lukewarm about her. Perhaps when she should meet the one to whom she could give her heart, she would give it with a passion that would shake every fibre of her little body. This was the reason why she was restless in her betrothal to Orito.

She instinctively felt her capability for a deeper love. The Japanese are not, as a rule, a demonstrative people. It is said to be a weakness to love before marriage, though a great many do so, especially those who are thrown into contact with the opposite sex to any extent. Numè knew this, and strove bravely to live up to the popular idea. She did not, as yet, understand her own self, nor was she cognizant of the possibilities for feeling which were latent in her. She attributed her restlessness solely to the fact that she was so soon to be married. She had not analyzed the word "love." It had only existed in her vocabulary since she had known the Americans. She had tired Mrs. Davis out asking questions about it. "Was this luf good?" "Was it wrong to luf too many people?" "Why must she not tell when she lufed any one?" "Did the pretty Americazan ladies luf their husbands, and was that why they were always so proud and beautiful?" "She" (Numè) "would like to luf too."—"How would she know it?"

These almost unanswerable questions, and many others, she put to Mrs. Davis, that lady answering them as sagely and wisely as possible, the natural love of romance prompting her to encourage the girl to talk so, but her desire to give only such advice as would keep her from thinking of Sinclair causing her to modify her answers so that they might suit the case. The worst of the matter was that although Numè would thank her very sweetly for any information on the subject, she had a lingering doubt that she ever wholly believed her, and that, in spite of her advice, the girl would willfully permit her thoughts to run riot. No! the Americazan lady could not prevent Numè from thinking of whom she chose.

XXXIV

Conspirators

This visit to Mrs. Davis' house broke the retirement Omi and Numè had planned for themselves. Besides, the girl was tired of the seclusion, and wanted to go out once more. And Omi had lost a good deal of the old interest in his daughter that he had had before Orito had told him of his love for the American girl. He was still very strict with her, at times; but soon he got into the habit of neglecting her, and would go over to the house of Sachi, where the two old men would sit mournfully together, neither of them alluding in any way to their children; so that Numè was left a great deal to herself, and allowed to do pretty much as she liked. She and Koto would start out in the mornings with their lunches in tiny baskets, and would spend the entire day on the hills, or the shores of the Hayama, wandering idly in the cool shade of the trees, or gathering pebbles and shells on the shore. Sometimes they would join parties of young Japanese girls and boys, who came up to the hills from a little village near there. They were the children of fishermen, and were plump and healthy and happy. Numè and Koto would play with them as joyously as if they, themselves, were children.

One day when Numè and Koto were in the woods alone together, and Numè had made Koto tell her over and over again of the gay life of the geisha girls in Tokyo, Numè said:

"Koto-san, let us some day go up to Tokyo alone. Lots of girls now travel alone, and we are so near the city. We would not let my father know, and as he is away with Takashima Sachi all day, he would never miss us. No one will recognize us in the city, or if they do they'll think we are there with some friends, but it is common for two girls to be together in the city, is it not, Koto?"

Koto said it was, but looked a trifle scared at this proposal. However, she was as eager as Numè to carry it out, for they had both grown very tired of the quietness of their life; especially Koto, who was used to the noisy city. She entered into the project at once.

"Let me go first to the city alone to-morrow," she said, "and I will tell your father that I have business to do there; then I will go and make arrangements at a jinrikisha stand to send a special vehicle to meet us each day—or every other day."

"And will we see Shiku?" Numè asked.

Koto's face beamed.

"If you say so, Numè-san—if you will permit."

"Why, of course I will," Numè said, excitedly. "Where will we see him?"

"I will tell him to meet us. He works for the American consul, and he is very good to Shiku."

Numè looked at her narrowly.

"Do you know, Koto-san, that the American consul is the Mr. Sinka I tell you of?"

"No; Shiku calls him only 'master sir,' and 'the consul.'"

Numè was silent a moment.

"And will we see the consul also, Koto?"

"Oh, no! because if we do not want any one to know we must be very careful not to be recognized."

So the two girls planned, and the next day Koto went up to the city and made every arrangement.

XXXV

A Respite for Sinclair

It was about two weeks later. Orito had not returned from Yokohama, neither had Cleo Ballard returned from Matsushima. She was enchanted with the beauty of the wonderful bay, and after the strain she had been under in Tokyo, it was a great relief for her to be away from the noise of the city in a spot that suggested only beauty and rest.

Sinclair had not accompanied them on the trip. He had been somewhat surprised at the haste in which it had been undertaken, and had told Cleo that unless he could travel leisurely he did not care to go at all; besides, he never enjoyed traveling with a large party of tourists, preferring to go alone with one congenial companion. However, he urged her to go, saying that he might run down himself and join them in a few days.

After the departure of the party he was left almost entirely to himself. He found time for looking about him. It was a relief for the time being to feel free once more, and to come and go as he chose; whereas, when the Ballards were in the city, he had always felt in duty bound to be with them constantly, and to place himself and his time entirely at their disposal. Sinclair was not looking well. He had grown thin and nervous, and there was a harassed look about his usually sunny face. Sinclair was by no means an extraordinary or brilliant man. He was easy-going in disposition, a trifle stern and harsh to those he disliked, but as a rule genial and easy to get on with. He was a favorite both with men and women. He was too good-natured to be a strong man, perhaps, and was easily swayed by his own likes and dislikes.

His engagement worried him more than he cared to admit. He told himself constantly that he ought to be happy, that nine men out of ten would have envied him Cleo. He recognized that she was good and generous, as well as beautiful; but yet all this seemed rather to paralyze his efforts to love her than otherwise. He knew her beauty and charms too well. When a man admits to himself that he has summed up all a woman's charms, then be sure affection begins to wane; for where there is love the lover is constantly discovering new charms, and, in fact, even those he has known are ever new to him.

Sinclair was weary. The prospect of his marriage appalled him. Even the beauty of the country, in which he had hitherto taken such great delight, ceased to interest him. It was replete with sadness now. The girl's departure was an unconscious respite and relief to him.

After they had left he threw himself into the actual joy of living, which life in Japan always suggests. He succumbed to the *dolce far niente* of the atmosphere, went out into the country, with his Japanese interpreter and office boy, and even on two or three occasions visited the tea-houses and frivolled away a few dreamy hours with the light-hearted geishas.

Often he and an English traveler named Taylor would find a quiet spot on the Hayama, where they would spend the entire day fishing, a favorite pastime of Sinclair's. Shiku would accompany them, carrying their rods and the Englishman's sketching apparatus, for in a quiet, unobtrusive fashion Taylor was quite a clever artist, though he painted almost entirely for his own pleasure. He would often desert the rod for the brush and leave Sinclair to fish alone, while he tried to reproduce parts of the exquisite, incomparable landscape; for, as some clever Japanese poet has described the scenery in Japan, it consists of "precious jewels in little caskets," and that within the vicinity of Fuji-Yama, from many points of which a distant view of the peerless mountain can be seen, is one of the most beautiful of all the lovely spots in Japan.

Taylor was of an uncommunicative, reticent nature,—strong and staunch. Between the two men an inexplicable friendship had sprung up, one that partook of no confidence betwixt them, but showed itself simply in the pleasure they took in being together.

XXXVI

THOSE BAD JINRIKISHA MEN

O ne balmy day in June, when the woods were so still that scarce a leaf stirred on the branches of the trees that shaded a spot along the Hayama where the two friends were fishing and smoking together, they were aroused from a pleasing silence by voices on the road which ran curving along the river bank only a short distance from where they sat. They were women's voices, and they were raised in protest. The Englishman lazily puffed on at his pipe, saying laconically:

"Some damned jinrikisha man, I suppose. Got a nasty habit, some of them, of demanding extra fare of women when they get them well on the road, and then, if they don't pay, won't carry them any further."

The American turned to Shiku:

"Go and see what you can do, Shiku."

Shiku ran lithely through the small bush that separated them from the road. After a time he came back, his face flushed and indignant.

"The lady has forgot to bring more money than the fare, and now the runners will charge more."

Sinclair stopped watching the line at the end of his rod. He put his hand carelessly into his trousers pocket, pulling out a handful of small change. "How much is it, Shiku?"

"Fifteen sen."

"Here you are."

"Wait a moment," said the Englishman, slowly, pulling in his line. "I'll just step over with you, and punch his head for him."

Sinclair smiled to himself as he watched his tall, strong figure disappear among the trees. As he did not return for some time, Sinclair also drew in his line, and sauntered toward the road. Taylor was not bullying the runners. Instead, he was listening very attentively to the little Japanese women in the jinrikisha, who seemed tearful and excited. As Sinclair came nearer to them he caught what one of them was saying:

"An' I bring no *more* moaneys." The halting English struck him with a pleased ring of familiarity. He turned sharply to look at her face. It was Numè!

XXXVII

THOSE GOOD JINRIKISHA MEN

It did not take Sinclair long to learn the source of her trouble. It seems she and Koto had been making trips to Tokyo, and had made special arrangements with a jinrikisha man to take them for so much per week. Unfortunately, two new runners had been given to them that day. Like the rest of their class, they were unscrupulous and, consequently, as soon as they were in a portion of the road from which the girls could not attempt either to walk to the city or to their home, they had stopped to demand extra fare. This the girls could not pay them, having no more with them. Thereupon the runners had refused to carry them farther. It was in this pitiful plight the two men had found them.

Sinclair reprimanded the men very severely, threatening to report them to the police, as soon as he returned to Tokyo. He could not be too harsh, however, because at heart he was thanking them for giving him this happy chance to see Numè again.

How pretty she looked in the soft kimona! He had only seen her in conventional American evening dress. It had seemed to him, then, wonderfully lovely and suited to her; now he thought it incongruous when compared to the Japanese gown on her.

"You must have been awfully frightened," he said; "better stop a while until you are composed;" then, as the girls hesitated, "I'll fix it all right with the runners." He did so, and soon all were in good humor. As for Numè and Koto, they stepped daintily, almost fearfully, from the jinrikisha, and followed the two men to the pretty shaded spot, leaving the jinrikisha men with their vehicles to take care of themselves.

Sinclair noticed that the Englishman seemed to know Numè. He addressed her as Miss Watanabe, and inquired after Mrs. Davis.

"You have met before, I see," he remarked.

"Ess," the girl smiled; and Taylor repeated the incident of how he had spoken to her father of the girl's beauty.

"Did I offend you?" he asked the girl.

"Ess."

Both Sinclair and Taylor laughed heartily at her assent, and the two girls joined in, scarcely knowing what they were laughing at, but feeling strangely happy and free.

Numè called their attention to Koto, telling them she was her friend and maid. Sinclair recognized the girl almost immediately as she smiled at him.

"And so you have been making almost daily trips to Tokyo?" he said, wondering at the girl's skill in evading detection.

"Ess—we become so *lonely*."

"Well, it's a jolly shame to shut you up like they do the women here," Taylor said, with a vivid memory of how the girl had been kept under such rigid seclusion after his conversation with her father. Taylor began fumbling with his sketching tools.

"Will you let me paint you, Miss Numè?" he asked. "I'll make the sky a vivid blue behind you, and paint you like a bright tropic flower standing out against it."

The girl looked at Sinclair standing behind Taylor. He shook his head at her.

"No," she said, with exaggerated dignity, "Numè does not wish to be painted."

"Well, what about Koto?"

Koto nodded her head in undisguised pleasure at the prospect.

XXXVIII

Disproving a Proverb

While Taylor sketched Koto, Sinclair and Numè wandered away from them, and finding a pretty shady spot sat down together. The girl was strangely shy, though she did not pretend to hide the artless pleasure she had in seeing him again.

"What have you been doing with yourself all these days, Numè?"

"Nosing."

"I thought you had been making sly trips to Tokyo?"

"I was *so lonely*," the girl said, sadly.

"You ought to be very happy now—now that your marriage is assured."

"Numè is nod *always* habby," she answered, wistfully. "Sometimes I tell Mrs. Davees I am nod *vaery*, Vaery habby, an' she laf at me, tell me I donno how habby I am."

"But why are you not always happy?"

"I *don't* to understand. I thing' thad I want to—" she looked Sinclair in the face with serious, wistful eyes—"I thing' I want to be luf," she said.

Sinclair felt the blood rush to his head in a torrent at this strange, ingenuous confession. The girl's sweet face fascinated him strangely. He had thought of her constantly ever since he had met her. With her strange, foreign, half-wild beauty, she awakened in him all the slumbering passion of his nature, and at the same time, because of her sweetness, innocence and purity of heart, a finer sense of chivalry than he had ever felt before—a wish to protect her.

"You do not need to wish to be loved, Numè—every one who knows you must love you."

"Koto luf me," she said, "tha's all. My fadder *vaery* proud of me sometimes, an' thad I marry with Orito; Orito luf me a liddle, liddle bit—Mrs. Davees—vaery good friend—you—" she paused, looking at him questioningly. Then she added, shyly:

"You are *vaery* good friend too, I thing'."

Sinclair had forgotten everything save the witching beauty of the girl at his side. She continued speaking to him:

"Are you habby, too?" she asked.

"Sometimes, Numè; not always."

"Mrs. Davees tell me thad you luf the pretty Americazan lady all with your heart, an' thad you marry with her soon, so Numè thing' you *mus'* be vaery habby."

Sinclair made a nervous gesture, but he did not answer Numè. After a while he said:

"Numè, one does not always love where one marries."

"No—in Japan naever; bud Mrs. Davees say nearly always always in America."

"Mrs. Davis is wrong this time, Numè."

About a half hour later he heard Taylor calling to them.

"Numè," he said, as he helped her rise to her feet, "I know a pretty spot on the river not far from your home. Won't you and Koto come there instead of going all the way to Tokyo?"

The girl nodded her head. As they started up the hill she said: "Mrs. Davees tell me *not* to say too much to you."

"Don't put any bar on your speech, Numè. There is nothing you may not say;" he paused, "but—er—perhaps you had better not say anything to *her* about our meeting."

He was strangely abstracted as he and Taylor trudged back to their hotel. The Englishman glanced at him sideways.

"Nice little girl, that—Numè-san."

Taylor stopped in the walk to knock the ash from his pipe against a huge oak tree.

"Hope she is not like the rest of them."

"What do you mean?"

"Ah—well, don't you know—lots of fire and all that—but as for heart—ever hear the old saying: 'A Japanese flower has no smell, and a Japanese woman no heart'?"

The perfume-laden blossoms and flowers about them stole their sweetness into his nostrils even as he spoke. Perhaps Sinclair recognized this.

"It is doubtless as untrue of the woman as the flower. Ah—pretty good smelling flowers those over there, eh?" He plucked a couple of wild flowers that resembled the pink.

"Well, I guess the poet—or—fool—who said that alluded only to the national flower—the chrysanthemum," Taylor said.

"Apparently—yes; he was a fool;—didn't know what he was talking about."

XXXIX

Love!

S ummer in the woods—summer in Japan! Ah! the poet Hitomaru sang truly over a thousand years ago, when he said: "Japan is not a land where men need pray, for 'tis itself divine." It seemed as if the Creator had expended all the wealth of his passion and soul in the making of Nippon (Japan) the land of beauty. It pulsated with a warm, wild, luxuriant beauty; the sun seemed to shine more broadly over that fair island, kissed and bathed it in a perpetual glow until the skies and the waters, which in their clearness mirrored its glory, became as huge rainbows of ever-changing and brilliant colors. Color is surely contagious; for the wild birds, that sang deliriously, wore coats that dazzled the eye; the grass and flowers, the trees and blossoms were tinged with a beauty found nowhere else on earth; and even the human inhabitants caught the spirit of the Color Queen and fashioned their garments to harmonize with their surroundings. So, also, the artists of Japan painted pictures that had no shadows, and the people built their houses and colored them in accord with nature.

What spirit of romance and enchantment lurked in every woodland path, every rippling brook or stream! Sinclair was intoxicated with the beauty of the country. It is true he had lived there nearly three years now, but never had it struck him as being so gloriously lovely. Why was there an added charm and beauty to all things in life? Why was there music even in the drone of the crickets in the grass? Sinclair was in love! Love, the great beautifier, had crept into his heart, unseen. Numè knew it—knew that Sinclair loved her. From the first he had never even tried to battle against the growing love for Numè which was consuming him, so that he thought of nothing else, night or day. His letters to Cleo Ballard grew wandering and nervous, or he did not write at all to her. He would neglect official business to meet Numè on the banks of the Hayama, and spend whole days in her company, with no one by them save the wee things of nature, and within call of Koto and Shiku. Neither did Numè struggle against or make any resistance. With all the force of her intense nature she returned his love. And it was the awakening of this love in her that had taught her to be discreet. She had taken the lesson well to heart that Mrs. Davis had taught her—to tell no man she loved him even if she did love him.

"Orito is coming home neg's weeg," she told him one morning.

Sinclair drew his breath in sharply.

"It will mean, then, the end of our—our happy days in the woods."

Numè was feeling perverse. Why did not Mr. Sinka tell her he cared for her—did he love the beautiful American lady more than he did her?

"Oh, no—*not* the end, Mr. Sinka," she said; and added, cruelly, "Orito can come, too."

It was the first time she had ever seemed to trifle with him. Hitherto she had always been so gentle and lovable. He felt a pain at his heart, and his eyes were quite stern and contracted.

"Numè," he said, almost harshly, "you—you surely hold our meetings more sacred than that. You know they would lose their essence of happiness and freedom, with the intrusion of a third party."

The girl was filled with remorse, in an instant.

"Ess, Mr. Sinka," she said. "Please forgive bad Numè."

"Forgive you, Numè!" He turned his eyes reluctantly from the girl's flushed face. "Oh! little witch," he whispered, holding her hands with a passionate fierceness. "You tempt me so—tempt me to forget everything save that I am with you."

She let her hands rest in his a moment. Then she withdrew them and rose to her feet restlessly. Sinclair rose also, looking at her with yearning in his face.

"Why do you speag lig' thad, Mr. Sinka?" she asked.

"Numè, Numè, don't you understand—don't you know?"

"No! Numè does *not* onderstand Americazan. Mrs. Davees tell me thad the Americazan genleman mag' luf to poor liddle Japanese women, but he nod really luf—only laf at her."

A cold anger crept over Sinclair.

"So she has been telling you some more yarns?"

"No; she telling thad yarns long, long time ago."

He recovered himself with an effort.

"I won't make love to you, Numè," he said, bitterly. "You need not fear."

In his misery at his helplessness and inability to tell the girl how much he loved and wanted her, he was doubting her,—wondering whether it were indeed the truth that a Japanese woman had no heart. A feeling of utter misery came over him as he thought that perhaps

Numè had been only playing with him, that her shy, seeming pleasure in being with him was all assumed. He looked down at the girl beside him. Perhaps she felt that look. She raised her little head and smiled at him, smiled confidently, almost lovingly. His doubts vanished.

"Numè—Numè!" was all he said; but he kissed her little hands at parting with a vehemence and passion he had never known.

XL

A Passionate Declaration

K oto," Numè said that night, as the maid brushed her hair till it shone bright and glossy as the shining jade-stone she placed before the huge Buddha when she visited the Kawnnon temple, "Mr. Sinka luf me."

"I know," the other said, quite complacently, and as though she had never had even the smallest doubt about it.

"Why, Koto," Numè turned around in surprise, "how do you know?"

"Shiku tell me first. He say always the august consul carry with him the flowers you give him, and he leave his big work for to come and see you."

Numè smiled happily.

"Do you think he will love me forever, Koto?"

"Ah, no!" Koto answered, elaborately; "because the august consul is to marry with the honorably august American woman in two months now, and of course he love only his wife then."

This answer displeased Numè. She spoke quite sharply to Koto. "But he tells me love never dies; that when he will love somebody he love her only forever."

Koto shrugged her shoulders.

"Americans are very funny. I do not understand them."

The next day Numè asked Sinclair whether he thought it possible for one who was married to love any one else besides his wife.

"Yes, Numè, it is possible," he said.

Then an idea struck him that she was thinking of her own case and her approaching marriage to Orito.

"I don't believe in such marriages," he said. "I would despise a woman who loved one man and married another." Numè smiled sadly.

"Ah, Mr. Sinka, that's *vaery mos'* sad thad you despising poor liddle womans. Will you despise *also* grade big mans who do same thing?"

Then Sinclair comprehended. His face was quite haggard.

"Oh, Numè, Numè-san," he almost groaned, "what can I do?" The girl was silent, waiting for his confidence.

"You understand, Numè, don't you—understand that I love you?"

The girl quivered with his passion, for a moment, then she stood still in the path, a quiet, questioning, almost accusing, little figure.

"But soon you will marry with the red-haired lady," she said.

"No! I cannot!" he burst out, passionately. "I won't give you up! Numè, I—I will try to free myself. It must not be, now. It would be wronging all of us. Sweetheart, I never cared for her. I never loved any one in the world but you, and I think I loved you even that first night. I will tell her all about it, Numè. She is a good woman, and will give me my freedom. Then she will go back to America, and we will be married and be together here—in this garden of Eden." He was holding her little hands in his now, and looking into her face hungrily.

"Think of it, Numè," he repeated; "only you and I together—always together—no more parting at the turn of the road—no more long, long nights alone. Oh! Numè! Numè!"

"But Orito?" she said, with pitiful pain. "Ah! my father would surely kill me. You dunno my people."

"Yes, I do, sweetheart. You must tell them—they will forgive in time—promise me, Numè—sweetheart."

He drew her towards him, but the girl still held back.

"Wait," she cried, almost in terror. "We *mus'* be sure firs' *thad* my father, *thad* Orito will not killing me."

"Kill you!" the man scoffed at the idea.

"Bud Numè is afraid," she persisted, and pulled her little hands desperately from his. She ran a little way from him, a sudden feeling of shyness and terror possessing her.

"Koto!" she called.

At the bend of the road where they were wont to part Sinclair helped her into the waiting jinrikisha. Her little hand rested against his sleeve for a moment. She was not afraid now—now that Koto was with her, and the runners were watching them. She was not afraid to let him read her little heart now. Such a look of tenderness and love and passion was in her small flower face as filled Sinclair with a wild elation.

"My little passion flower," he whispered, and bending kissed her little hand fervently.

XLI

A Hard Subject to Handle

When the girls reached their home that afternoon they found Mrs. Davis waiting for them. Numè, who thrilled with a joy she herself could not comprehend, ran to her, and putting her arms about her neck, clung with a sudden passion to her.

"Oh, Numè is so habby," she said.

Mrs. Davis undid the clinging arms, and looked the girl in the face. Then Numè noticed for the first time that the American lady was unusually silent, and seemed almost offended about something. Numè tried to shake off the loving mood that still lingered with her, for where one is in love there is a desire to caress and shower blessings everywhere, and on all living creatures. So it was with Numè.

"I want to have a talk with you, Numè dear," Mrs. Davis, said, gravely; and then turning coldly to Koto she added, "No, not even Koto must stay." The little maid left them together.

"Numè, how could you be so sly?"

"Sly!" the girl was startled.

"Yes—to think that all these weeks when you have been pretending to be alone with Koto in the woods, you have been meeting Mr. Sinclair."

The girl turned on her defiantly.

"I nod telling you account tha's nod business for you."

"Well, Numè!"

"I getting vaery lonely, and meeting only by accident with Mr. Sinka."

"Does your father know?" the other asked, relentlessly.

The girl approached her with terror. "No! Oh, Mrs. Davees, *don't* tell yet." After a time she asked her: "How did *you* know?"

"I learned it by accident through a clerk at the consulate. How he knows—and how many others know of it, I cannot say." She almost wrung her hands in her distress. She saw it was no use being angry with Numè, and that she might do more by being patient with her. She had learned merely the fact of Sinclair's being in the woods each day with a Japanese girl. This had set her to thinking; Koto's and Numè's long absences in the country each day—a few questions and a handful of sen to the runners who had been loitering in her vicinity for some days now with their vehicles, and she soon knew the truth.

Just how far things had gone between Sinclair and Numè she must find out from the girl herself, though she was not prepared to trust her completely when she realized how Numè had deceived her all these weeks. She was determined to help Cleo, and felt almost guilty when she remembered that she had urged the girl to make the trip which might result in so much disaster to her, for Jenny Davis knew Cleo Ballard well enough to know that it would break her heart to give Sinclair up now, after all the years she had waited for him.

"Numè," she said, quite sadly, "don't look at me so resentfully. I want only to do my duty by you and my friend. Let me be your friend. Oh! Numè, if you had confided in me we could have avoided all this."

Numè had a tender spot in her heart for Mrs. Davis, who had always been so good to her.

"*Forgive* Numè," she said, impulsively, and for a moment the two women clung together, the American woman almost forgetting, for the moment, everything save the girl's sweet spontaneity and impulsiveness. Then she pulled herself together, remembering Cleo.

"Numè, tell me just what—just how—all about the—the meetings with Mr. Sinclair."

The girl shook her head, flushed and rebellious.

"Me? I *nod* tell. Mr. Sinka tell me—all *too saked*."

Mrs. Davis caught her breath.

"He told you—told you the—the—meetings were sacred?"

Numè nodded:

"Ess."

"Then he is not an honorable man, Numè, because he is betrothed to another woman."

"Bud he writing her to breag'," the girl said, triumphantly.

"He write to—Numè, what are you talking about? Are you conscienceless? When did he write—what?"

"He say he writing soon, and I telling Orito, too."

The girl's complacency cut Mrs. Davis to the quick. She forgot all about Cleo's flirtations. She remembered only that Cleo was her dearest friend—that this strange Japanese girl might cause her immeasurable trouble and pain, and that she must do something to prevent it.

"Numè, you can't really care for—for Sinclair."

"Ess—I luf," the girl interrupted, softly.

"Come and sit at my knee, Numè, like—like you used to do. So! now I will tell you a little story. How hot your little head is—you are tired? No? Oh, Numè, Numè, you have been a very foolish—very cruel little girl." Nevertheless, she bent and kissed the wistful upturned face.

XLII

A Story

O nce there was a young girl," Mrs. Davis began, "who was born in a beautiful city away across the seas. She was just as beautiful and good—as—as you are, Numè. But, although the city was very beautiful in which she lived, she had very little in her life to make her happy. She lived all alone in a house so big that the halls and stairways were as long as—as the pagodas. She seldom saw her father because he was always away traveling, and, besides, he did not love children much. Her mother was always sick, and when the little girl came near her she would fret and worry, and say that the little girl made her nervous. So she grew up very, very hungry for some one to love her. After a time, when she became a beautiful young lady, many men thought they loved her; but she had grown so used to not loving, and to not being loved by any one, that she never could care for any of them. At last there came one man who seemed different to her from all the others. And, Numè, he fell in love with her—and she loved him. Oh! you don't know how much they loved each other. They were with each other constantly, and, and,—are you tired?" she interrupted herself to ask the girl, who had moved restlessly.

"No."

"Well, Numè, then her lover, that she loved so much you would have cried to have seen her, went far, far away from her to take a fine position, and he promised her faithfully that he would love only her, and would send for her soon. So the girl waited. But he did not send for her soon, Numè. He kept putting off and putting off—till three long years had passed; and all this time she had been true to him—waiting for him only to say the word to come. Then, at last, he wrote to her, asking her to come to him all the way across the seas—thousands and thousands of miles, and she left her beautiful home, and came with her sick mother to join him."

Numè's eyes were fastened on her face with a look of intense interest.

"Ess?" she said, as the American lady paused.

"When she reached him she found he had changed—though she had not. He was cold, and always bored; kind to her at times, and indifferent at others. Still, she loved him so much she forgave him, and was so sweet and gentle to him that even he began to melt and began to be kinder to her, and all, Numè, would have turned out happily, and he would have loved her as he used to, only—only—" she paused in her story. She had exaggerated and drawn on her imagination strongly in order to make an impression on Numè; for she knew the girl's weakness lay in her tender heart.

"*Only* whad, Mrs. Davees?"

"Numè—the girl was Miss Ballard—the man Mr. Sinclair. Oh, Numè, you don't want to separate them now after all these years. Think how cruel it would be. It would kill her, and—"

Numè had risen to her feet. She looked out at the burning blaze of the oriental landscape, the endless blue of the fields—at the misty mountains in the distance. She was trying to reason. The first real trouble of her life had come to her. She thought of all to whom she would bring sorrow should she yield to Sinclair; of the two old fathers, for she knew nothing as yet of what Orito had told them. She thought of the beautiful American girl, and remembered the look on her face that night of the ball. She wondered how she would have felt in her place. Her voice was quite subdued and hushed as she turned to Mrs. Davis.

"Numè will marry *only* Orito," she said. "Numè will tell Mr. Sinka so."

The other woman put her arms around the girl and attempted to draw her to her with the old affection; but Numè shrank strangely from her, and perhaps half the pleasure at her success was lost as Mrs. Davis saw the look of mute suffering in the girl's face.

XLIII

The Truth of the Proverb

It was with a heart full of yearning and love that Sinclair waited for Numè the next day. She was late; or was it that that last look of hers had turned his head so that he had come earlier than usual to the spot, unable to wait the appointed time?

He found himself planning their future together. How he would love her—his bright tropic flower, his pure shining star—his singing bird. Every leaf that stirred startled him. He tried to absorb himself in the beauty of the country, but his restlessness at her failure to come caused him to go constantly to the road and see if there were any signs of her.

At last he heard the faint, unmistakable beat, beat, beat of sandaled runners. They started his blood throbbing wildly through his veins. She was coming—the woman he loved, the dear little woman who had told him she loved him—not in words—but with that last parting, sweet look; and oh! Numè was too sweet, too genuine, too pure, to deceive.

As he helped her from the jinrikisha and looked at her with all his pent-up longing and eagerness, she turned her head aside with a constrained look. Koto stayed close by her, and refused to take any suggestion from Sinclair to leave them alone together.

Numè began to talk hastily, and as though she could not wait.

"We have had lots of fon, Mr. Sinka?"

"Fun!—why, Numè!"

She opened her little fan and shaded her face a moment.

"Ess—Numè and all Japanese girl luf to have fon."

"Numè—I don't like that word. It is inapplicable in our case."

He tried to take her hand in his, but it clung persistently to her fan, while the other remained hidden in the folds of her robe.

"My little girl is quite cross," he said, thinking she was trying to tease him.

"No! Numè nod mos' *vaery* cross;" after a moment she added, in a hard voice: "Numè does nod *want* to have any *more* fon." She clung to that word persistently.

"You do not want any more fun, Numè!" he repeated, slowly; "I don't understand you."

"Ess—it is *all* fon," she said. "All fon thad we pretending to luf."

"All fun?" he echoed, stupidly. "What is all fun, Numè? Why, what is the matter, sweetheart—why so contrary to-day?"

"Nosing is madder 'cept that Numè does nod wand any more fon with you—she tired *vaery* much of Mr. Sinka."

A silence, tragic in its feeling, passed between them.

"What do you mean, Numè?" He was still stupid.

"That I only have fon to pretend that I luf you—I am very tired now."

A gray pallor had stolen over the man's face.

"You—you are trying to jest with me, Numè," he said unsteadily.

The truth began to dawn on him gradually. He remembered his doubts of the former day. He had been deceived in her after all! Oh! fool that he was to have trusted her—and now—now he had not thought himself capable of such fierce love—yet he loved her in spite of her deceit, her falsity.

He got up and stood back a little way from her, leaning against a tree and looking down at her where she sat. A sudden wild sense of loss swept over him. Then his voice returned—it was muffled and unfamiliar even to his own ears.

"Numè!" was all he said; but he stretched his arms toward her with such yearning and pain that the girl rose suddenly and ran blindly from him, Koto following. On, and on, to where the jinrikisha was waiting. Koto helped, almost lifted her bodily in, and as the runner started down the road, Numè put her head back against Koto and quietly fainted away.

When she came to herself she was in a high fever. She called pitifully for Sinclair, begging Koto to take her to him—to go to him and tell him that she did not mean what she had said; that she was trying to help Mrs. Davis; that she loved only him, and a thousand other pitiful messages. But Mrs. Davis had her carried to her house and stood at her bedside, invincible as Fate.

Sinclair remained where she had left him for some time, the same dazed expression on his face. When the girl had darted from the fallen tree on which they had sat, she had dropped something in her flight. Mechanically he stooped and picked it up. It was a Japanese-American primer. Numè and he had studied out of it together. He ground his teeth with wild pain, but he threw the book from him as if it had been poison. He ran his hand through his hair, tried to think a moment, and then sat down on the fallen tree, his face in his hands.

There Taylor and Shiku came across him, sitting alone, looking out at the smooth, scintillating waters of the Hayama.

"Had a sunstroke, old man?" Taylor asked.

"No;" he rose abruptly to his feet. "I—I was just thinking, Taylor—just thinking—thinking of—of what you had told me a month or so ago. Do you remember—it was about Japanese women?"

"Er—yes, about them having no heart. Remember we decided the poet—or fool, we called him—was wrong."

"He was wrong only about the flower, Taylor."

XLIV

NUMÈ BREAKS DOWN

A few days later Orito returned to Tokyo. His father's house was strangely sad and gloomy. On his return home from America it had been thrown open, as if to catch every bright ray of light and happiness. Now it was darkened. Sachi no longer sat in the little garden, but he and Omi were indoors trying to pass the time playing a game which resembled checkers.

Neither of them greeted Orito otherwise than sadly, both of them letting him see in every way that he had wounded them deeply, although Omi was a trifle hopeful and often told Sachi that he had great hopes that Orito would change his mind, that something would turn up to help them. Sachi, on the other hand, was inconsolable. Moreover, he was growing quite old and feeble, and this last disappointment seemed to have stooped his shoulders and whitened his hair even more.

Orito tried to cheer them up, telling them of some clever business deal he had made in Yokohama, by which he had sold a large tract of land for a good round sum.

"How is Numè?" he asked.

The old man shook his head sadly.

"Quite sick," he said. "She grew very sad and lonely for a time, and about a week ago she broke down when out with her maid, and was carried to Mrs. Davis' house, where she has been ever since."

"I'll go right over and see her," Orito said, with concern.

He found Numè looking very thin and wan. She was lying on an English sofa. Koto was beside her, singing very softly as she played on her samisen. Orito paused on the threshold, listening to the last weird, thrilling notes of the beautiful song, "Sayonara" (Farewell).

"It is indeed very sad to find you sick, Numè," he said, gently, as he sat down beside her.

She smiled faintly.

"I am afraid you have kept too much in seclusion, Numè. You ought to go out more into the open air."

Still the girl smiled silently—a pitiful, trembling, patient smile.

Mrs. Davis came into the room and welcomed Orito, trying to cheer the girl up at the same time. "Now we will get better soon," she said, pinching the girl's chin—"now that Orito has come home."

"Ess," the girl answered, vaguely. "Numè will be bedder now."

Koto laid her face against the sick girl's, caressing her little head with her hand.

"Your voice is so weak, Numè-san," she said.

A look of genuine sympathy and affection passed between mistress and maid. Koto understood her, if no one else did. Koto loved her and would stand by her through thick and thin.

Orito expressed himself to Mrs. Davis as being very shocked to find Numè so weak and thin. He had not heard of her illness. How long had it been?

"Only a few days," Mrs. Davis told him. It had been very sudden. She would improve soon, now that Orito had returned.

Her persistency in dwelling on the fact that it depended on him— the restoration of Numè's health—irritated Orito. He knew Numè better than Mrs. Davis imagined; and knew, also, that she did not love him so that for the sake of it she would suddenly break down and become as white and frail as a lily beaten by a brutal wind.

Koto talked to him rapidly in Japanese. She wanted them to return home soon. Neither she nor Numè were comfortable. "Numè wanted to be all alone with Koto, where no one—not even the kind Americans— could intrude until she should be better again."

"I will carry her across the fields now," Orito said, and told Mrs. Davis of his intention of doing so. That lady seemed very anxious that the girl should not be removed for several days. But Numè settled the question by rising up from the couch and saying she was perfectly strong, and wanted to return home; that she would always be grateful for the kindness Mrs. Davis had shown her, but would Orito *please* take her home?

The American lady was in tears. She kissed the girl repeatedly before letting her go, but Numè was too listless to be responsive.

Ever since that day when she had fainted in the jinrikisha and had awakened in a high fever, Numè had been sick—ill with no particular malady, save perhaps the strain and shock.

Mrs. Davis had been very kind to her, waiting on her with her own hands, once staying up all night with her. In fact, she and Koto had vied with each other in serving and doing everything to please her, but

Numè seemed to have lost interest in everything. The only thing that soothed her was for Koto to sing and play very gently to her, and this the little maid did constantly.

XLV

Trying to Forget

S inclair had become suddenly attached to his work. He deserted the
country for the city, remaining sometimes quite late in the evening
in his office, attending to certain matters that had collected during his
absences from the office. One was the case of an American missionary
who had been arrested for attempting to bribe school boys to become
Kirishitans (Christians). The charge against him was that he had caused
dissension in several of the public schools by bribing certain of the
poorer children to leave their schools, and, in some cases, their homes,
and attend the missionary school in Tokyo. It was said that he had
become a terror to parents in the district, who were afraid of losing their
children, for he generally got them to accompany him by paying them
small sums of money.

One deserter who had been converted to the Christian belief by
a bright silver yen, was accredited with having told him after he had
become a backslider and the missionary had reproached him: "You pay
me ten more sen I go to church—you pay me twenty sen I love Jesus."

On the other hand, the missionary declared he had merely interfered
and protested at the harsh treatment Christian children received at the
hands of their playmates in the schools, and which he declared was
encouraged by the teachers. In this way he had antagonized some bitter
Japanese against him, who had had him unjustly arrested and thrown
into prison.

The case was quite a serious one, as the missionary was a well-known
man in America. It gave Sinclair plenty of thought and work, and he
was untiring in his endeavor to obtain his discharge.

He had seen nothing of Numè since that day in the woods, when she
had told him she had never cared for him. In spite of constant visitors
and the volume of his work, which he tried personally to superintend
for the time being, Sinclair could not forget Numè. The moment he
was left to himself his mind would revert to the girl, to the dreamy days
he had spent with her in the woods, to little things she had said that
lingered in his mind like Japanese music. In spite of himself he could
not hate her. Had she been an ordinary woman it might have been

different, but with Numè could he cherish anything harsher against her than regret?

He tried to assure himself that he had put her from his mind altogether, that after all she was unworthy of his pain, but every incident that came up which reminded him of her, found him wandering back to the dear dead days he had spent with her, days that were tinged with bitterness and regret now.

XLVI

AN OBSERVANT HUSBAND

So, though Sinclair tried honestly to forget Numè and harden himself against her, he could not do so. He grew so thin and wretched looking that his friends began to notice it. They thought it was due to the fact that he had worked so hard lately on the missionary's case.

"You ought to take a rest and change of some sort, Sinclair," Mr. Davis told him, "now that you have got the missionary off. Why not take a run down to Matsushima, where the Ballards are? Cleo thinks the spot even more beautiful than about Fuji-Yama."

"I hadn't thought of going away," Sinclair said, absently; "besides, Cleo is coming back next week, anyhow."

"Well, suppose you run down for the rest of the week, and then come home with the party."

Sinclair remained thinking a moment.

"Yes, perhaps it would divert me for the time being," he said, drawing his brows together with a sudden flash of pain, as he remembered how he had once told Numè that they would visit Matsushima together, some day. Mr. Davis left him at his desk.

"Can't make out what's the matter with Sinclair," he told his wife. "He looks wretched, and is as absent-minded as he can be. Seems to be worrying about something."

"He no doubt is—a—lonely, Walter. When Cleo returns he will be all right."

In the same way as she trusted or tried to make herself believe that Orito's presence would cure Numè, so she liked to imagine that Cleo Ballard's return would raise Sinclair out of the despondency into which he had fallen.

"No—Jenny, I think you make a mistake about Sinclair's caring so much for Cleo," Walter Davis said, slowly.

"What makes you say that?" his wife interrupted, sharply, fearful that he had guessed something during Numè's illness in their house; for she had told him nothing, as yet.

Her husband hesitated a moment before answering, then he said:

"Fact is, I saw on his desk quite a batch of unopened letters. I wanted

Sinclair to go somewhere with me. He pleaded press of business, and I took it he had to answer those letters. They were all from one person, Jenny, and were lying in a letter basket on his desk without even the seals broken. I made the remark that he had quite a lot of mail for one day. What do you think he answered? 'This is nearly a week's mail'—and said he had forgotten the letters."

Davis flicked the ash from his cigar into a receiver, then he continued, slowly: "My dear, the letters were from Cleo Ballard. I know her writing. A man does not let the letters from a girl he is in love with remain unopened long," he added.

Mrs. Davis got up. "Walter," she said, indignantly, "that man is a—a brute."

XLVII

Matsushima Bay

Matsushima Bay is perhaps one of the most beautiful spots in Japan. It is on the northeastern coast, and being cool and refreshing is a favorite summer resort. Countless rocks of huge size and form are scattered in the bay, and these rocks are covered with pine trees. Unnamed flowers bloom also on these rocks and burn their surface with flaring colors. It may be that the rocks are even more nutritious than the earth itself; for the tall pines that take their root in them seem more graceful and delicate than those found on land, and the flowers are more fragrant and lovely than those of a fairyland dream.

About eight miles from the northern shore, where rests the beautiful city of Sendai, towers Mount Tomi, only a shadowy tracing in the evening skies.

It was in the city of Sendai that the party of tourists had settled. They were charmed with the beauty of their surroundings, and being, most of them, ardent lovers of nature, made daily trips, exploring the country, visiting the temple Zuiganji, which is located only a few cho from the beach. This temple originally belonged to Marquis Date, the feudal lord of Sendai, who sent an envoy to Rome in the seventeenth century, and a wooden image of him still stands in the temple. Or they climbed Mount Tomi in order to get a view of the matchless bay with its countless white rocks; eight hundred and eight, they are said to number, and there is only one rock in the entire bay which is bare of foliage. It is called Hadakajima, or Naked Island.

Sinclair arrived in this ideal, quiet, restful spot, travel-stained, sick-hearted and weary. Some of his travel had been by rail, a great part solely by kurumma. He had sent Cleo Ballard no word of his proposed trip, and he was not expected. She was not at the hotel when he arrived, having gone out with her party to the mountains.

Sinclair went immediately to the room assigned him, and after bathing went to bed in the middle of the day. He had not slept for several days, in spite of the strange lassitude and weariness he had felt. The inviting white of the American bed tempted him. It was perhaps the first real sleep he had had in weeks.

When the party of tourists returned to the hotel the clerk told Cleo Ballard of the arrival of a gentleman who had enquired for her. A glance at the register showed her Arthur Sinclair's name.

Fanny Morton and a number of women acquaintances were at her elbow. After the first start of emotion and surprise she tried to appear calm before them and as if she had expected him.

"So he has arrived?" she said carelessly to Tom—and to the clerk: "Please send him word that we have returned."

The boy brought the answer back that the American gentleman was sleeping—they did not like to wake him.

"He must be very tired," the girl said.

Sinclair did not appear in the dining-room that evening. His dinner was served to him in his room, and Cleo Ballard saw nothing of him till the following day.

"I am so glad you have come, dear," she told him; "the summer was going by so quickly, and I was afraid you had forgotten your promise."

"Did I make any promise," he asked, indifferently.

"Why, of course, Arthur;" she looked hurt.

"Well, I forgot, Cleo. One can't remember all these little things, you know."

"Then what made you come?" she asked, sharply, stung by his indifference.

"Not because of any promise, my dear," he said. "Simply because I was tired," and then as he saw her hurt face he added, with forced gentleness: "I wanted to see you—that was the chief reason, of course."

Cleo melted.

"You know, dear," she said, "we had arranged to go back to Tokyo the end of this week. Of course we will postpone our return, now, on your account. You really must see the country with us."

"Well, Cleo, I have seen Matsushima before. I only wanted a change for a day or two, that was all. No; don't delay the return home—as—I—," he struck some gravel aside with his cane; "the fact is, it is too quiet here, and I prefer the city."

The party returned to Tokyo about a week later, Sinclair feeling somewhat better. The bracing air, the beauty of the bay, and the constant companionship of friends, served to turn his mind, for a time, from his troubles.

XLVIII

A Rejected Lover

S inclair found a very odd letter waiting for him on his return to Tokyo. It was written in English, and ran as follows:

Tokyo, August 20, 1896
Hon. A. Sinclair

Dear Master Sir:

Here I write to you ashamed to say to below lines.

I intend to marry in next month soon as I get money. I must spend two hundred yen while I marry. My father gave me fifty yen upon day before yesterday, and I was have twenty yen on my hands. I have already seventy yen at present, and I know extraly some of my friends will help me.

Anyway, soon I shall have full one hundred yen, but I cannot begin marrying with that much money, so I complain to you for borrow me some money if you like that I going to marry. If you thinking right and borrow me some in this time, I will be thousand thanks for you until before I die. Afterward I will pay back to you as soon as I can, but I cannot pay you all in one time. I would pay six yen each end of per month.

Although this is not great bisiness for you, but as for me first greatly bisiness in my life. If you do not like to borrow me some money in this time I never marry in before several years.

Do as you please that you like it or not.

I have very many things to tell you, but I know English very little so I stop.

Your lovely (loving) clerk,
Shiku

Sinclair read the letter aloud to Taylor, and both of them laughed heartily, enjoying the contents; then he touched the electric button on his desk. The next minute Shiku was with them.

"So you want to marry, Shiku?"

"Yaes, master-sir."

"Um! Have you settled on the girl yet?"

"Yaes, master-sir."

"Fortunate girl!" from Taylor.

"And you think she'll have you?"

"Yaes, master-sir."

"What's her name?"

"Tominaga Koto."

"Not Koto whom I painted in the woods?" put in Taylor.

The boy nodded his head sagely.

Sinclair had grown suddenly silent. The mention of Koto's name instantly called up memories of Numè—memories that he had told himself, when at Matsushima with Cleo Ballard, would no longer cause him a pang. His voice was quite gentle as he spoke to Shiku.

"Well, go ahead and marry her, Shiku. I'll make you a gift of the money, and perhaps a trifle more."

The boy thanked him humbly, repeating over and over that he was a thousand thanks to him until before he died.

"Rum little chap that," Taylor said, as the boy left them.

"Yes, he *is* a bright little fellow. Been with me now ever since I came to Japan."

"Well, he's going to get a mighty pretty girl."

"Yes—I suppose so—as good as the rest of them."

The next day Shiku presented himself before the consul with a very woe-begone and disappointed countenance.

"Well, Shiku, what luck?" Sinclair asked him. For the boy had gone straight to Koto.

"Koto will not marry with me, master-sir."

"Why, I thought you told me she had already promised."

"Yaes—bud—she changing her mind."

Sinclair laughed, shortly.

"Been fooling you?"

"No;" he hesitated a moment, as though he feared to tell Sinclair the truth. Then he said: "She not like for to leave her mistress now;—" he paused again, looking uneasily at the consul, and shifting from one foot to the other.

Sinclair had been opening some letters with a paper-cutter while the boy had been speaking. He suddenly laid it down, and wheeled round on his chair.

"Well?"—he put in.

"Numè-san is quite sick," the boy said.

"Quite sick!" Sinclair rose with an effort. He was struggling with his desire to seem indifferent, even before the office boy, but a sudden feeling of longing and tenderness was overpowering him. It shocked him to think of Numè's being ill—bright, happy, healthful Numè.

"What is the matter?" he asked.

"I not know. Koto say she cry plenty, and grow very thin,—that she have very much luf for somebody."

"Ah!"

"I tell Koto," the boy continued, "that I think she love Takashima Orito, and that he not love her she is very sad."

Sinclair began to pace the floor with restless, unsteady strides.

"Yes—it's doubtless that, Shiku," he said, nervously. "Well, I'm sorry—sorry that your—that your marriage will have to wait."

XLIX

The Answer

The same day that Sinclair had heard of Numè's illness, Cleo Ballard received a letter from Orito. It was very brief and simple.

"I am coming to see you," it ran, "at seven o'clock to-night, before your party will start. Then will I ask you for the answer you promised me."

Mrs. Davis was with her when she received the letter.

"Now, you *must* be strong, my dear," she said. "See him, and have it all over."

"Yes, I will," Cleo Ballard said.

Precisely at seven o'clock Takashima Orito presented himself at the hotel. He had told his father and Omi of his mission there; and the two old men were waiting in great trepidation for his return.

As he stood, calm but expectant, by the girl's side, waiting for her to speak first, she felt a sudden fear of him. She did not know what to say. She knew he was determined to have a direct answer now.

"I don't know what to say." She broke the strained silence desperately.

"I have only one answer to expect," he said, very gently. This answer silenced the girl. The Japanese came closer to her and looked full in her face.

"Will you marry with me, Miss Cleo?"

"I—I—" She shrank back, her face scared and averted.

"I cannot!" she said, scarcely above a whisper.

She did not look at him. She felt, rather than saw, that he had grown suddenly rigid and still. His voice did not falter, however.

"Will you tell me why?" he asked.

"Because—I—am already betrothed—to Mr. Sinclair. Because I never could love any one but him."

The shadows began to darken in the little sitting-room. The Japanese was standing almost as if petrified to the spot, immovable, silent. Suddenly she turned to him.

"Forgive me," she said, and tried to take his hand.

He turned slowly and left the room without one backward look.

The silence of the room frightened her. She went to a window and put her head out. A sudden vague terror of she knew not what seized her. Why was everything so still? Why did he leave her like that? If he only had reproached her—that would have been better;—but to go without a word to her! It was awful—it was uncanny—cruel. What did he intend to do? She began to conjure up in her mind all sorts of imaginary terrors. She told herself that she hated the stillness of the Japanese atmosphere; she wanted to go away—back to America, where she could forget everything—where, perhaps, Sinclair would be to her as he had been in the old days. She had been on a nervous strain all day, and she broke down utterly.

Mrs. Davis found her walking up and down the room hysterically.

"There, dear—it is all over now,"—she put her arms about the girl and tried to soothe her.

"No, no, Jen; I feel it is not over. I think—I imagine—Oh, Jenny, I don't know what to think. He acted so queerly. I don't know what to think. I dread everything. Jenny," she put her hand feverishly on the other woman's shoulder, "tell me about these Japanese—can they—do they feel as deeply as we do?"

"Yes—no; don't let's talk about them, dear. Remember, they are giving you and the travelers a big party to-night at the hotel. You *must* dress—it is nearly eight now."

L

THE BALL

Never had Cleo Ballard appeared so beautiful as that night. Her eyes shone brightly with excitement, her cheeks were a deep scarlet in hue, and her wonderful rounded neck and arms gleamed dazzlingly white against the black lace of her gown.

Even Sinclair roused out of his indifference to look after her in deep admiration.

"You are looking very beautiful to-night, Cleo," he said; and ten minutes afterwards Tom, passing with Rose Cranston on his arm, laid his hand on Cleo's shoulder: "You are looking unnaturally beautiful, Cleo. Anything wrong?"

"Must there necessarily be something wrong, Tom, because I am looking well?"

Tom gave her a scrutinizing glance. In spite of her quick bantering words there was something in the girl which made him think she was laboring under some intense excitement, and that it was this very excitement that was buoying her up and lending her a brilliancy that was almost unnatural. Tom knew the reaction must come. All through the evening he watched his cousin. She was surrounded almost constantly, save when she danced. Later in the evening he pushed his way to her side. She was resting after a dance.

"Cleo, you are dancing too much," he said, noting the girl's flushed cheeks.

"One can't do anything too much, you know, Tom. I hate moderation in anything—I hate anything lukewarm;" she was answering at random. He put his hand on hers. They burned with fever.

"You are not well at all," he said, and then added, looking about them anxiously: "I wonder where Sinclair is?"

The girl was possessed with a sudden anger.

"Don't ask *me*, Tom. I would be the last person to know of *his* whereabouts." The words were very bitter.

"You know, Cleo," he answered her, soothingly, "Sinclair never did care for this kind of thing. He is doubtless in the grounds somewhere. Wait—I'll hunt him up." He rose from his seat, but the girl stayed him peremptorily.

"Not for *my* sake, Tom. Oh, I assure you, I shall not wither without him," she said.

Tom sat down beside her again.

"Look here, little sis, don't get cynical—nor—nor untruthful. I know very well you want to see Sinclair. I have not seen you together all evening, and I believe it's partially that which makes you so restless. No use trying to fool old Tom about anything."

Cleo did not argue the point any longer, and Tom passed on to the piazza of the hotel.

Quite a lot of the guests were congregated there, some of them telling tales, others listening to the music. Tom made his way to where he saw Mrs. Davis standing. She was with Fanny Morton, and they seemed to be waiting for some one.

August is the universal month for holding banquets in honor of the full moon, in Japan, and gay parties of pleasure-seekers are to be met on the streets at all hours of the night.

"Seen Sinclair anywhere about?" Tom asked them.

"Yes, Tom," Mrs. Davis said, nervously. "He and Walter went down the street for a while. Something has happened. Mr. Sinclair thought some one had got hurt. They said they would be back in a minute."

Tom waited with the two women. The dance music floated out dreamily on the air, mingled with the incessant chatter and laughter of the guests. Inside the brilliantly-lighted ball-room the figures of the dancers passed back and forth before the windows.

As they sat silently listening, and watching the gay revelry, a weird sound struck on their ears—it was the muffled beating of Buddhist drums.

The two women and Tom rose to their feet shivering. They turned instinctively to go indoors. Standing quite near the door by which they entered was Cleo. Her beautiful face was flushed with fever; her eyes were filled with terror. She was leaning forward, listening to the faint, muffled beat of the drums.

"Some one is dead!" she said, in a piercing whisper, and threw her beautiful bare arms high above her head as she fell prone at their feet.

LI

The Fearful News

What awful premonition of disaster had filled Cleo Ballard all that night! The guests gathered awestruck about the fallen figure which, but a moment before, was so full of life, vivacity, and beauty.

"What is the matter?" some one breathed.

Fanny Morton's sharp words cut the air:

"Some Japanese has died, that is all—killed himself, they say. She fainted when she heard the drums beat."

Very gently they carried the unconscious girl to her room. The music had ceased; the guests had lost their appetite for enjoyment. Almost with one accord all, save a few stragglers, had deserted the ball-room, and were now grouped in the grounds of the hotel, or on the steps and piazzas, waiting for the return of the two men who had gone to learn the cause of the alarm.

At last they came up the path. They walked slowly, laggingly. Mrs. Davis ran down to meet them.

"What is it?" she whispered, fearfully. "Cleo has fainted, and a panic has spread among all the guests."

Walter Davis's usually good-tempered face was bleached to a white horror.

"Orito, his father, and Watanabe Omi have all killed themselves," he said, huskily.

The American lady stood stock-still, staring at them with fixed eyes of horror. The news spread rapidly among the guests, all of whom had known both families well. They were asking each other with pale lips—the cause? the cause?

Mrs. Davis clung in terror to her husband.

"Keep it from Cleo," she almost wailed. "Oh, don't let *her* know it—she must not know it—she must not."

The guests lingered late that night, in the open air. It was past three o'clock before they began to disperse slowly, one by one, to their rooms or their homes.

LII

The Tragedy

After leaving Cleo Ballard, Orito had jumped into the waiting kurumma, and had been driven directly home. There he found the two old men waiting for him. The house was unlighted, save by the moonlight, which was very bright that night, and streamed into the room, touching gently the white heads of the two old men as they sat on their mats patiently awaiting Orito's return. It touched something bright, also, that lay on a small table, and which gleamed with a scintillating light. It was a Japanese sword!

Orito entered the house very silently. He bowed low and courteously as he entered the room, in strict Japanese fashion. Then he began to speak.

"My father, you have accused me sometimes of being no longer Japanese. To-night I will surely be so. The woman of whom I told you was false, after all." His eyes wandered to the sword and dwelt there lovingly. He crossed to where it lay and picked it up, running his hand down its blade.

"I have no further desire to live, my father. Should I live I would go on loving—her—who is so unworthy. That would be a dishonor to the woman I would marry for your sakes, perhaps. Therefore, 'tis better to die an honorable death than to live a dishonorable life; for it is even so in this country, that my death would atone for all the suffering I have caused you. Very honorable would it be."

Sadly he bade the two old men farewell; but Sachi stayed his arm, frantically.

"Oh, my son, let thy father go first," he said.

One thrust only, in a vital part, a sound between a sigh and a moan, and the old man had fallen. Then quick as lightning Orito had cut his own throat. Omi stared in horror at the fallen dead. They were all he had loved on earth, for, alas! Numè had represented to him only the fact that she would some day be the wife of Orito. Never, since her birth, had he ceased to regret that she had not been a son. He picked the bloody sword up, and with a hand that had lost none of its old Samourai cunning he soon ended his own life.

About an hour after this a horror-stricken servant looked in at the room in its semi-darkness. He saw the three barely distinguishable dark forms on the floor, and ran wildly through the house, alarming all the servants and retainers of the household. Soon the room was flooded with light, and the dead were being raised gently and prepared for burial, amidst the lamentations of the servants, who had fairly idolized them. Relatives were sent for in post haste, and before the night had half ended the muffled beating of Buddhist drums was heard on the streets, for the families were well known and wealthy, and were to be given a great and honorable funeral. And also, the sounds of passionate weeping filled the air, and floated out from the house of death.

LIII

A Little Heroine

It was three days later. Cleo Ballard had been sick with nervous prostration ever since the night of the ball. Mrs. Davis was with her constantly, and would permit no one whatever to see her—not even Sinclair. She had told the facts to her husband and to the doctor, and had enlisted them on her side; so that it was not a difficult matter for her, for the time being, and while Cleo lay too ill to countermand her orders, to forbid any one from intruding, for she did not want her to know of the awful tragedy that had transpired.

Sinclair inquired day and night after Cleo's health, and sent flowers to her. He, himself, had suffered a great deal since that same night, what with the shock of his friend's death, Cleo's unexpected illness, and, above all, an inexplicable longing and desire to see Numè—to go to her and comfort her in this fresh trial that had come to her. She was now utterly alone in the world, he knew, save for one distant relative.

Thoroughly exhausted with the trials of the last days, and wishing to get away from the hotel, Sinclair had shut himself indoors, and had thrown himself on a couch, trying vainly to find rest. He kept puzzling over the cause of Takashima's death. Whether the truth had been suspected among some of the Americans who had been on the boat with Cleo and Orito or not, no one had as yet breathed a word of it to him. As he lay there restlessly, some one tapped on his wall.

"Who is it?" he called, fretfully.

"It is Shiku, master-sir."

"Well, come in."

The boy entered almost fearfully, and began apologizing profusely in advance.

"It is Koto who has made me intrude, master," he said. "She is waiting outside for you, and tells me she must talk with you. She will not enter the house, however, and she is very much fearful."

The American went to the door. There stood Koto, a trembling, frightened little figure in the half-light.

"Come in, Koto," he said, noting her embarrassment; and then, as she still hesitated, he drew her very gently but firmly into the house and closed the door. Soon she was seated in one of his large chairs, and because she was such a little thing it seemed almost to swallow her up.

"Numè not know that I come tell you of our grade sadness," she said, stumblingly. "Mrs. Davis will not forgive me forever, but I *come* tell you the trute, Mister Consul." She began to weep all of a sudden, and could go no further. The sight of the wretched little sobbing figure touched Sinclair very deeply. He thought she had some revelation to make about the death of Orito. He was unprepared for her next words.

"My mistress, Numè-san, luf vou so much that she going to die, I thing'."

Sinclair stood up, a strange, doubting, uncomprehending look on his face.

"What do you mean, Koto?" he asked, sternly. "Are you trying to—to fool me about something?"

"No! No! I not to fool with you. I tell you the trute. Mrs. Davis tell Numè of *vaery* sad story account the august Americazan lady wait long many years for you, that you love her always, just not love for a liddle while, because of Numè, that—"

A sudden light began to break in on Sinclair.

"So Numè tell you *she* not to luf because she want to *serve* the honorable Americazan ladies and not to *pain* her father and Takashima Sachi. Then she get *vaery* sick. She cry for you all the time, and when she is very sick she say: 'Koto, go tell Mr. Sinka I not mean.' Then when she is better she say: 'No; Koto must not go.'"

Sinclair sat down again, and shaded his face with his hand. His mind was in confusion. He could not think. Only out of the jumble of his thoughts came one idea—that Numè loved him, after all. Now he remembered how unnatural, how excited, she had been that last day. Ah, what a fool he was to have believed her then!

His voice was quite unsteady when he broke the long silence. "Koto! Koto! how can I ever repay you for what you have done?"

The little maid was weeping bitterly.

"Ah! Koto is *vaery* 'fraid that she tell you all this, account Mrs. Davis will speag that I mus' not worg any longer for Numè; she will tell her relatives so, and they will send me away. Then Numè will be all alone; because only Koto love Numè forever."

Sinclair was smiling very tenderly. "You have forgotten me, Koto. I will take care of both of you, never fear, little woman. I am going with you to her now."

"It is too late now," the girl said. "Numè will have retired when we reach home. Shiku is going to take me home, and to-morrow will you come?"

She rose from her seat, looking more hopeful and happy than when she had first come in.

"You will make it all good again," she said, looking up at him with somewhat of Numè's confidence: "for you are so *big*."

LIV

Sinclair Learns the Truth at Last

After Koto had left Sinclair he sat down to think. His brain was whirling, for his thoughts and plans were in confusion. His first impulse had been to go straight to Numè; but he had promised Koto to wait until the following day. Now that he was alone, he suddenly remembered Cleo Ballard. Was he free to go, after all? Could he desert Cleo now while she lay so sick and helpless? His joy in the renewed assurance of Numè's love for him had been suddenly tinged with bitter pain. What could he do?

He slept none through the night. In the morning of the next day he hurried over to the hotel and made his usual enquiries after Cleo's health. Mr. and Mrs. Davis, with Tom, had done their best to prevent him from knowing the cause of Orito's suicide. Various reasons had been suggested; and after the first alarm had worn off, and the bodies had been interred with due ceremony, the excitement subsided somewhat, so that they had hopes of the talk quieting down, and perhaps dying out altogether, without the truth reaching Sinclair's ears; for, knowing him to be her betrothed, there were few who were unkind or unscrupulous enough to tell him.

As Sinclair passed through the hotel corridor on his way to the front door, Fanny Morton came down the wide staircase of the hotel. She stopped him as he was going out.

"*Let* me express my sympathy," she said, sweetly.

"Your sympathy!" he said, coldly; for he did not like her. "I do not understand you, Miss Morton."

"Yes," she cooed. "I am sure I can vouch for Cleo that she *never* dreamed he would take it so seriously. I was with them on the voyage out, you know, and indeed Cleo often said the passengers were dull. *He* cheered her up, and—and—"

"Really, Miss Morton, I am at a loss to understand you," he said, curtly.

Fanny Morton showed her colors. There was no suggestion of sweetness in her voice now.

"I mean that every one knows that Mr. Takashima killed himself because he was in love with Miss Ballard; because she let him believe on the boat that she reciprocated his—affection, and the night of the ball she told him the truth. He killed himself, they say, hardly an hour after he had seen her."

Jenny Davis stood right at the back of them. She had heard the woman's venomous words, but was powerless to refute them. Sinclair felt her eyes fixed on him with an entreaty that was pitiful.

He raised his hat to Fannie Morton.

"I will wish you good morning," he said, cuttingly, and that was all. Then he turned to the other woman.

"Let us go in here," he said, and drew her into a small sitting-room.

"What does that woman mean?" he asked.

Mrs. Davis had broken down.

"We can't keep on pretending any longer, Mr. Sinclair. Yes; it is true, what she says. Poor Cleo did lead him on, thoughtlessly—you know the rest."

A look of dogged sternness began to settle on Sinclair's face.

"Then she was the real cause of—"

"No! no! *don't* say that. Arthur, she never intended doing any harm. Cleo would not willingly harm anything or any one. She really liked him. Tom will tell you. It was the reason why she never had the heart to tell him—of—of her engagement to you."

For a long time the two sat in moody silence. Then Sinclair said, almost bitterly: "And it was for *her* that Numè suffered."

"Why, Numè—is—what do you mean?" the other asked, showing signs of hysteria.

"Yes; Mrs. Davis, I know the truth," he said, grimly. "I understand that you thought you were really serving Cleo and myself by acting so—but—well, a man is not cured of love so easily, you know. She (Numè) gave me up because she did not want to spoil a good woman's life, as she thought, after what you told her. This same woman did not scruple to take from her the man who might have comforted her after everything else had failed. Now she is utterly alone."

"I won't say anything now," Mrs. Davis said, bitterly. "I can't defend myself. You would not understand. It is easy to be hard where we do not love;—that is why you have no mercy on Cleo."

"I am thinking of Numè," the man answered.

"May I ask what you intend to do?"

"Last night I was uncertain. This morning, now that I know the truth, things are plain before me. I am going to Numè," he added, firmly.

"But Cleo?" the other almost implored.

"I cannot think of her now."

"But you will have to see her. What can you tell her? We are hiding from her, as best we can, the fact of—of the tragedy. *That* would kill her; as for your ceasing to care for her, she suspected the possibility of it long ago, and might survive that. Yet how can she know the one without the other?"

Sinclair remained thinking a moment.

"There is only one way. Let her think of *me* what she will. You are right; if possible the truth—even Takashima's death—must be kept from her so long as she is too weak to bear the knowledge. Can we not have her make the return voyage soon? I will write to her, and though it will sound brutal, I will tell her that the reason why I cannot be more to her than a friend is—because I—I do not love her,—that I love another woman."

Mrs. Davis was weeping bitterly. All her efforts and plans had been of no avail in Cleo's behalf. She saw it now, and did not even try to hold Sinclair.

"Yes," she said, almost wildly. "Go to Numè—she will comfort you. At least your sorrows and hers have ended, now. But as for ours—Cleo's and mine, for I have always loved her better than if she were my own sister—we will try to forget, too."

LV

Lovers Again

Koto had told Numè nothing of her visit to Sinclair. The girl had been so stunned by the deaths of her father, Orito, and Sachi, that Koto had not the heart even to tell her good news; for when our friends are in sorrow the best comfort one can give is to weep and sorrow with them;—so the Japanese believe. Besides, she wanted Sinclair's coming to be a surprise to the girl.

In Numè's great sorrow and illness she would have no one by her save Koto, and once in a while Koto's friend, Matsu, who was visiting them. Koto had had her come to the house because she played the harp so beautifully, and she knew the music would please Numè. Both the girls tried in every way to make up to the grieving orphan for the sorrows that had suddenly come to darken her young life. Often the three would sit together hand in hand, Numè between her two friends, speaking no word to each other, but each feeling strangely comforted and refreshed with the others' love and sympathy. After the funeral ceremony, Numè had awakened somewhat out of her apathy, and tried to take interest in things about her; but it was a pitiful effort, and always made Koto weep so much that one day Matsu had suggested to her that she go to the city and see the American and tell him the truth. For Numè had told Koto of what Mrs. Davis had caused her to do; and Koto, in her turn, had told Matsu.

"You have become too secluded and proud, Koto," the city geisha girl told her. "It is an easy matter to go to the city and perhaps you will do Numè and the American a great service. I will stay with Numè-san while you are gone, and will wait on her just as if I were indeed her maid instead of your being so." It was in this way Koto had been induced to visit the American.

The next morning, as she and Numè sat together, she said:

"Numè-san, did you know why Orito killed himself?"

"No."

"It was because he loved the honorable American lady."

Numè did not interrupt her. Koto continued: "The beautiful one that was betrothed to Mr. Sinka."

Numè's little hands were clasped in her lap. She did not speak, still.

Koto went on: "You see, she was not worthy, after all, that you sacrificed the pretty American gentleman for her, for Matsu says that all the Americans say at the hotel that she tell Orito sometime that she love him just for fun—and she not love—so Takashima Orito kill himself."

Still Numè did not reply. Her little head had fallen back weakly against the pillow. She was looking away out before her. After a time Koto put her arms about her, and they clung together.

"Koto," Numè said, vaguely, "will you leave me now? Or will you stay with me forever? Numè is so lonely now."

Koto evaded the question.

"I will stay with you, Numè-san, until you do not need me any longer."

"That will never be," the other said, tenderly.

That afternoon Koto fetched her samisen and played very softly to Numè. After a time she laid her instrument aside and went to the door, shading her face with her hand as she scanned the road. It was about the hour Sinclair had told her to expect him. She heard the beat of his runners before they were within a mile of the house.

"I am going to leave you all alone, for a little while," she told Numè.

She went down to meet Sinclair, and admitted him into the house. She pointed to the room where Numè was and then left him.

Sinclair pushed aside the shoji and passed into the room.

Numè raised her head languidly at the opening of the screens. At first she thought she was dreaming, and she sat up straight on the little couch on which she had been resting. Suddenly Sinclair was beside her, and had taken her bodily into his arms.

"Numè! Numè!" he whispered;—and then, as she struggled faintly to be free, he said, blissfully, "Oh, I know the truth, little sweetheart, though it is too good for me to understand it yet. Koto has told me everything, and—and oh! Numè!" He kissed the wistful eyes rapturously.

He scarcely knew her, she had grown so quiet and sad. In the woods she had chattered constantly to him;—now, he could not make her say anything. But after a while, when Sinclair had chided her for her silence, she said, very shyly:

"Do you luf me, Mr. Sinka, bedder than the beautiful Americazan lady?"

Sinclair raised her little face between his two hands.

"Sweetheart—do you need to ask?" he said. "I have *never* loved any one but you."

The girl smiled—the first time she had smiled in weeks. Her two little hands met round his neck, she rose on tiptoe. "Numè *lig'* to kees with you," she said, artlessly. There is no need to tell what Sinclair answered.

When the shadows began to deepen, he and Numè still sat together on the small lounge, neither of them conscious of time or place. They were renewing their acquaintance with each other, and each was discovering new delights in the other.

It was Koto who broke in on them. She had been in the next room all the time, and had watched them through small peep-holes in the wall.

She made a great noise at the other side of it to let them know it was now getting late. They looked at each other smiling, both comprehending.

"Koto is our friend *foraever*," Numè said.

"We will be Koto's friends forever," Sinclair answered.

LVI

THE PENALTY

When Sinclair returned to the city that night he sat down in his office and wrote a letter to Cleo Ballard. It was the most difficult thing he had ever done in his life. It told her briefly of his love for Numè. He felt he could not be a good husband to her so long as he loved another woman. It was better she knew it than to find it out after they had married.

Mrs. Davis gave it to Cleo when she thought her strong enough to bear the shock. She read it with white lips, her poor, thin hands trembling as the letter slipped to her feet.

"I expected it," she said, bitterly, to Mrs. Davis; and then suddenly, without the smallest warning, she leaned over and picked the scattered sheets from the floor and tore them into a thousand fragments with such fierceness that it frightened her friend.

After that day Mrs. Davis devoted herself more than ever to her friend, and scarce left her alone for a moment. A strange calm and quiet had come over Cleo. She would sit for hours by an open window, perfectly silent, with her hands clasped in her lap, looking out before her with large eyes which were dry of tears, but which held a nameless brooding.

Mrs. Davis tried in every way to cheer her up, but though she protested that she was not suffering, yet she could not deceive her friend who knew her so well.

"You *are* going to be happy, dear, and as soon as you are strong enough we'll make the voyage back. You didn't know I was going with you, did you? Well, dear," her sweet voice faltered, "*I* couldn't bear to stay here—after—after you were gone. We will all be happy when in America again. I believe that's what has made us all more or less gloomy. We have been homesick. Japan *is* all right, beautiful and all that—but, well, it is not America. We never *could* feel the same here." So she rattled on to Cleo, trying to take the girl's thoughts out of herself.

And then, one day, Cleo turned to her and told her very quietly that she knew everything.

Mrs. Davis gasped. "Everything!"

She looked at the girl's calm, emotionless face in horror. "And—and you—"

"I've known it some time now," the girl continued, grimly. She heard the other woman sobbing for her, and put her hand out and found the little sympathetic one extended.

"I know—know, dear, how you tried to hide it from me," she smiled faintly; "that could not be."

Mrs. Davis was mute. Cleo was an enigma to her now.

"I never guessed you knew."

"No? Mother told me. She did not mean to be cruel, but she was not well herself then, and she—she reproached me."

She rose suddenly to her feet, the same still, white look on her face that had come there when she had read Sinclair's letter. She turned on her friend with an almost fierce movement.

"Why don't you *hate* me?" she said, with only half-repressed vehemence. "Why does not every one—as I do myself?"

She was beyond the comfort of her friend now. Jenny Davis could only watch her with wide eyes of wonder and agony. For a moment the girl paced the room with restless, dragging step, like a wild caged thing.

"Jenny, I will tell you something now. You may laugh at me—laugh as—I can—as I do myself, but—" Again she paused, and she put her hand to her throat as though the words choked her.

"After I read that—that letter, it seemed as if something broke in me—not my heart—no, don't think that; but at first I felt desolate, with a loneliness you could never comprehend. He had been in my mind so many years then. Yes, I know—I had expected it all—but it was a shock at first. I never *could* face anything painful all my life, and when I actually knew the truth—when I read his letter, and it *was* cruel, after all, Jenny, I wanted to go away somewhere and hide myself—no—I wanted to go to some one—some one who really loved me, and cry my heart out. Don't you understand me, Jenny? Oh, you must—" her voice was dragging painfully now. "I wanted—to—go—to Orito!"

"Cleo!"

"Yes, it is true," she went on, wildly. "*He* was better than the other. So much tenderer and truer—the best man I ever knew—the only person in the whole world who ever really loved me. And I—Jenny, I *killed* him! Think of it, and pity me—no, don't pity me—I deserve none. And then—and then—" she was beginning to lose command of her speech now. Mrs. Davis tried to draw her into a chair, but she put the clinging, loving hands from her and continued: "When I wanted him—when that other had deserted *me*—had let me know the truth that he never did care for me—never did care for me," she repeated, incoherently, "and I loved him all those years. I used to lie awake at night and cry for him,—for Orito—for his comfort—just as I do now. I cannot help myself. I thought I would go to him and tell him everything—*he* would understand—how—how my heart had awakened—how I must have loved him all along. And then—then mother burst out at me only last week, Jenny, and told me the truth—that—that he was *dead*—that he had killed himself; no—that I had killed him. Do you wonder I did not *die*—go mad when I learned the truth? Oh, Jenny, I am half dead—I am so numb, dead to all pleasure, all hope in life."

She had been speaking spasmodically; at first with a hard, metallic ring to her voice, and then wildly and passionately. Now her voice suddenly trembled and melted. She was still quite weak, and had excited herself. Her friend caught her to her breast just in time for the flood of tears to come—tears that were a necessary, blessed relief. She broke down utterly and began to sob in a pitiful, hopeless, heart-breaking fashion.

From that day, however, she seemed to improve, though she was erratic and moody. She would insist on seeing all the callers—those who came because of their genuine liking for her, and sorrow in her illness, and the larger number who came out of curiosity. However much of her heart she had shown to Mrs. Davis, no one else of all Cleo's friends guessed the turmoil that battled in her breast.

LVII

The Pity of It All

Although it was nearly two weeks since Sinclair had written to her, she had not seen him once. He had talked the matter over with Tom and Mrs. Davis, and they had decided that, for a time at least, it would be best for her not to see him. About a week before the Ballards sailed, Cleo wrote to Sinclair. She made no allusion whatever to his letter to her. She simply asked him to come and see her before she left Japan, and without a moment's hesitation Sinclair went straight to her. He could afford to be generous now that his own happiness was assured.

It was a strange meeting. The man was at first constrained and ill at ease. On the other hand, the girl met him in a perfectly emotionless, calm fashion. She gave him her hand steadily, and her voice did not falter in the slightest.

"I want you to know the truth," she said, "before I go away."

"Don't let us talk about it, Cleo," Sinclair said. "It will only cause you pain."

"That is what I deserve," she said. "That is why I have always been wrong—I was afraid to look anything painful in the face. I avoided and shrank from it till—till it broke my heart. It does me good now to talk—to speak of it all."

He sat down beside Cleo, and looked at her with eyes of compassion.

"You must not pity me," she said, a trifle unsteadily. "I do not deserve it. I have been a very wicked woman."

"It was not altogether your fault, Cleo," he said, vaguely trying to comfort, but she contradicted him almost fiercely.

"It *was*—it was, indeed, all my fault." She caught her breath sharply. "However, that was not what I wanted to speak about. It was this. I wanted to tell you that—that—after all, I do not love *you*. That I—I loved *him*—Orito!" She half-breathed the last word.

Sinclair sat back in his chair, and looked at her with slow, studying eyes.

She repeated wearily: "Yes; I loved him—but I—did not—know—it till *it was too late*!"

For a long time after that the two sat in complete silence. Sinclair could not find words to speak to her, and the girl had exhausted her heart in that heart-breaking and now tragic confession.

Then the man broke the silence with a sharp, almost impatient, exclamation, which escaped him unconsciously. "The pity of it all!— Good God!"

"Arthur, I want to see—to speak to Numè before I go away. You will let me; will you not?"

He hesitated only a moment, and then: "Yes, dear, anything you want."

And when he was leaving her, she said to him, abruptly, with a sharp questioning note in her voice that wanted to be denied:

"I am a very wicked woman!"

"No—no; anything but that," he said, and stooping kissed her thin, frail hand.

Something choked him at the heart and blinded his eyes as he left her, and all the way back to his office, in the jinrikisha, he kept thinking of the girl's white, suffering face, and memories of the gay, happy, careless Cleo he had known in America mingled with it in his thoughts in a frightful medley. Something like remorse crept into his own heart; for was he entirely blameless? But he forgot everything painful when he arrived home, for there was a perfume-scented little note written on thin rice-paper, waiting for him, and Numè was expecting him that day. When one has present happiness, it is not hard to forget the sorrows of others.

LVIII

Mrs. Davis's Nerves

The next day Sinclair brought Cleo to call on Numè. It was the first time the two girls had ever really talked with each other. At first Numè declared she would not see the American girl, whom she held responsible for her father's, Sachi's and Orito's deaths, but after Sinclair had talked to her for a while and had told her how the other girl was suffering, and how she, after all, really loved Orito, the girl's tender little heart was touched, and she was as anxious to see Cleo as Cleo was to see her.

She went herself down the little garden path to meet Cleo, and held her two little hands out with a great show of cordiality and almost affection.

"Tha's *so* perlite thad you cummin' to see me," she said.

Cleo smiled, the first time in days, perhaps. It pleased Numè. "Ah!" she said, "how nize thad is—jus' lig' sunbeam in dark room!"

She was very anxious to please the American girl and make her feel at her ease, and she chatted on happily to her. She wanted Cleo to understand that in spite of her father's death she was not altogether unhappy, for she had talked the matter over very solemnly with Koto and Matsu only the previous night, and they had all agreed that Cleo's desire to see her (Numè) was prompted by remorse, which remorse Numè wished to lessen, to please Sinclair.

Sinclair left them alone together, and strolled over to Mrs. Davis's house. She had been kept in ignorance of this proposed visit. Sinclair found her busily engaged in packing, preparatory to leaving. Mrs. Davis was in despair over some American furniture that she did not want to take with her.

"Can't you leave it behind?"

"No; the new landlord won't let me. Says the Japanese have no use for American furniture—unpleasant in the houses during earthquakes, etc."

"Well, I'll take care of them for you," Sinclair volunteered, good-naturedly.

"Oh, will you? Now, that *will* be good of you. That settles that, then. And now about this stuff—come on, Tom," she began crushing things into boxes and trunks, in her quick, delightful fashion, scarce noting where she was placing them. She paused a moment to ask Sinclair if he had been over to Numè's.

"Yes," he smiled a trifle. "Cleo is there now."

She dropped a piece of bric-a-brac and sat down on the floor.

"Cleo! *there—with Numè!* Well!"

"Yes, she wanted to *know* Numè, she said, before going away," Sinclair told her.

"She will never cease surprising me," Mrs. Davis said, plaintively. "She ought not to excite herself. I never know *what* to expect of her, which way to take her. I used to think my nerves were strong; now—my nerves are—are nervous."

"Cleo is not herself lately," Tom said, quietly, without looking up. "We'd better humor her for a little while still. Besides—Numè will do her good, I believe."

LIX

CLEO AND NUMÈ

As soon as Sinclair left them the Japanese girl went close up to the American girl.

"Sa-ay—I goin' tell you something," she said, confidingly.

"Yes, dear."

"You mos' beautifoolest womans barbarian—No! no! nod thad. Egscuse me. I *nod* perlite to mag' mistakes sometimes. I mean I thing' you mos' beautifoolest *ladies* I aever seen," she said.

Again Cleo smiled. Numè wished she would say something.

"You lig' me?" she prompted, encouragingly.

"Yes—"

"Foraever an' aever?"

"Well—yes—I guess so."

"How nize!" she clapped her hands and Koto came through the parted shoji.

"*Now* I interducing you to my mos' vaery nize friens, Mees Tominago Koto."

Koto was as anxious as Numè to please, and as she had seen Numè hold her two hands out in greeting, she did the same, very sweetly.

About an hour later Mrs. Davis, with Tom and Sinclair, looked in at the three girls. Cleo was sitting on the mats with Koto and Numè, and they were all laughing.

"Well, we've come for the invalid," said Tom, cheerily. "She has been out long enough."

"I have enjoyed my visit," she told them, simply. "And Numè," she turned to her, "Numè, will you kiss me?"

"Ess;" she paused a moment, bashfully, throwing a charming glance at Sinclair. "I *kin* kees—Mr. Sinka tich me."

They all laughed at this.

"An' now," she continued, "I inviting you to visit with me agin." She included them all with a bewitching little sweep of her hands, but her eyes were on the American girl's face. "An' also I lig' you to know thad Mr. Sinka promising to me thad he goin' tek me thad grade big

United States. Now, thad *will* be nize. I egspeg you lig' me visite with you also. Yaes?"

"Of course; you would stay *with* us," Tom said, cordially.

"Thad *is* perlite," she breathed, ecstatically.

"Not polite, Numè," Sinclair corrected, smiling, "but, well—'nize,' as you would call it."

"Ah, yaes, of course. I beg pardons, egscuse. I mean thad liddle word 'nize.' Tha's foolish say 'perlite.'" She laughed at what she thought her own foolishness, and she was so pretty when she laughed.

Cleo turned to Sinclair. "I understand," she said, softly, "why you— you loved her. If I were a man I would too."

"Ah! thad is a regret," sighed Numè, who had overheard her and half understood. "Thad you nod a mans to luf with me. Aenyhow, I thing' I liging you without thad I be a mans. Sa-ay, I lig' you jus' lig' a—a brudder— no, lig' a mudder, with you." This was very generous, as the mother love is supreme in Japan, and Numè felt she could not go beyond that.

Cleo seemed very much absorbed on the way home. Tom was in the kurumma with her, Sinclair having stayed behind a while.

"Matsu is going back with us to America," she said. "I think she is a dear little thing, and I shall educate her." She was silent a moment, and then she said, very wistfully:

"Tom, do you suppose I can ever make up—atone for all my wickedness?" and Tom answered her with all the old loving sympathy.

"*I* never *could* think of you as wicked, sis—not wantonly so—only thoughtless."

"Ah, Tom—if *I* could only think so too!"

When the boat moved down the bay Cleo's and Tom's eyes were dim, and when the wharf was only a shadowy, dark line they still leaned forward watching a small white fluttering handkerchief, and in imagination they still saw the little doleful figure trying to smile up at them through a mist of tears.

And a week later the selfsame missionary who had given Sinclair so much work, and thereby helped him bear his trouble, married them— Sinclair and Numè. The girl was gowned all in white—the dress she had worn that first time Sinclair had met her.

About two years later a party of American tourists called on Sinclair. Among them were a few old acquaintances. They brought strange news. Cleo and Tom Ballard had been married for a month past!

Perhaps the most frequent visitors at the Sinclairs' are Mr. and Mrs. Shiku.

THE END

A Note About the Author

Winnifred Eaton, (1875–1954) better known by her penname, Onoto Watanna was a Canadian author and screenwriter of Chinese-British ancestry. First published at the age of fourteen, Watanna worked a variety of jobs, each utilizing her talent for writing. She worked for newspapers while she wrote her novels, becoming known for her romantic fiction and short stories. Later, Watanna became involved in the world of theater and film. She wrote screenplays in New York, and founded the Little Theatre Movement, which aimed to produced artistic content independent of commercial standards. After her death in 1954, the Reeve Theater in Alberta, Canada was built in her honor.

A Note from the Publisher

Spanning many genres, from non-fiction essays to literature classics to children's books and lyric poetry, Mint Edition books showcase the master works of our time in a modern new package. The text is freshly typeset, is clean and easy to read, and features a new note about the author in each volume. Many books also include exclusive new introductory material. Every book boasts a striking new cover, which makes it as appropriate for collecting as it is for gift giving. Mint Edition books are only printed when a reader orders them, so natural resources are not wasted. We're proud that our books are never manufactured in excess and exist only in the exact quantity they need to be read and enjoyed.

bookfinity™

Discover more of your favorite classics with Bookfinity™.

- Track your reading with custom book lists.
- Get great book recommendations for your personalized Reader Type.
- Add reviews for your favorite books.
- AND MUCH MORE!

Visit **bookfinity.com** and take the fun Reader Type quiz to get started.

Enjoy our classic and modern companion pairings!